THIRTEEN

An anthology of crime stories

Edited by: **M.H. Callway**
Donna Carrick
Joan O'Callaghan

CARRICK
PUBLISHING

D1194459

THIRTEEN

An anthology of crime stories
by the Mesdames of Mayhem

Edited by:
M.H.Callway
Donna Carrick
Joan O'Callaghan

Cover Art by Sara Carrick

Carrick Publishing

Print Edition 2013
ISBN 13: 978-1-927114-63-6

Kindle Edition 2013
ISBN 13: 978-1-927114-62-9

License Notes:

CARRICK
PUBLISHING

THIRTEEN

"Putting all of these award-winning, fun loving, criminal-minded (fictionally of course), feisty female writers in one anthology can't lead to anything but great reading, great laughs, and great trouble." ~ Anthony Bidulka, author of *When the Saints Go Marching In.*

"Before stepping out with these dangerous mesdames of criminal literature, be fully armed. Celebrated novelists and short-story writers such as Sylvia Warsh, Rosemary Aubert, and Canada's Queen of Comedy Melodie Campbell will make you an offer you can't refuse. Fifteen suspenseful tales are guaranteed to keep you turning pages until dawn." ~ Lou Allin, author of the *Belle Palmer mystery series.*

Table of Contents

Foreword

by M.H. Callway

A meeting place for deadly minds....

Welcome Readers!

Thirteen merry Mesdames of Mayhem have prepared a deadly mix of crime stories to entice, enthrall and ultimately terrify you. These wickedly crafted tales weave together intricate themes of mother love, age and revenge. Never again will you feel safe in a hallowed cathedral or a charming country church. There is no solace in a seemingly normal high school or a family's beloved cottage. Nor can you put your trust in police officers in July, or in history-loving librarians in small Ontario towns. And no one will hear you scream in that tough bar in outer space.

You would be wise to remember the saying about old age and cunning. In these pages, oldsters hunt fortunes, hoard cursed antiquities and engage in cross-border spying, not shopping. And they will stop at nothing to defend their neighbour's worms. Youth is no protection either. What's a newly-wed to do when her husband finds only dust, not gold? And there you are, planning the perfect wedding, when someone drops a body in your car—just because you happen to be the Goddaughter of a certain Italian family.

Nothing is as it seems. Senior civil servants stumble across lions…or do they? And black cats may or may not bring bad luck. You must enter these pages to find out.

The Mesdames of Mayhem are fifteen friends brought together through shared literary critique groups. All are published authors in the crime fiction genre. Many of the Mesdames have won crime writing awards, including the Edgar, Arthur Ellis, Indie and Bony Pete. Many more have earned nominations for these or other awards, such as the CWA's Debut Dagger.

To learn more about us, follow the links in these pages and visit our website at

http://mesdamesofmayhem.com/

Not My Body

by Melodie Campbell

"Gina, you have to have red flowers. Whoever heard of a Christmas wedding without red flowers?" Nico waggled a finger and shook his bleached blond head at me.

"Sweetie, I'd rather have pink. You can find pink poinsettias, right?"

He sat back and his brown eyes went wide. "Pink! My favorite! And black. It's perfect. I can see it now—black table cloths with ice sculpture centrepieces....pink poinsettias on those narrow platforms with streamers coming down from the ceiling…"

He was out for the count. I could sip my coffee in peace now. Not that there wasn't peace in this restaurant. It was Monday night and the place was only half full.

Nico is my younger cousin, an interior designer, newly minted. He is tall, thin and runs a design and event planning business next to my jewelry store in Hess Village. He is rather enthusiastic about my upcoming wedding. Some might say over-the-top.

Nico isn't gay—he just likes the colour pink. So I knew I could get him off the red Christmas kick with a little subterfuge.

We were seated at La Paloma, my uncle Vito's resto in the slick part of Hamilton. OK, don't laugh. The

Hammer has some nice places in amongst the steel mills. This upscale bistro was across the street from a major urban teaching hospital, so it's popular with doctors. Doesn't hurt that my other uncle, Vince, donated a whole wing to St. Mary's, and sits on the board.

Vince is also my godfather. You may have heard of him. Let me leave it at that.

"What do you think about peacocks?" Nico said.

I fumbled my coffee cup. "PEACOCKS?"

A crash from the kitchen punctuated that word.

Someone screamed.

"Aunt Vera?" Nico was out of his chair, dashing for the kitchen.

I threw down my linen napkin and jogged right behind him.

The kitchen staff stood like immovable stone statues. I had to push my way to the back, where Vito was standing in front of the open door to the alley.

Aunt Vera, Vito, Nico and I peered down at a body. It didn't move because it had been recently plugged.

"Ohmigod, Gina, I can't look. There's blood." Nico hid his face dramatically behind his bent elbow.

"Gina, do you know dis guy?" Aunt Vera poked at him with a wooden spoon.

"Who is it?" Nico said, peeking around his arm.

"Oh jeez. It's Wally the Wanker." Yeah, I knew him. Complete loser from high school. Pilfered the student lockers for cash and blackmail material. Even bigger creep in adult life. Not that Wally was ever an adult, except when it came to buying porn. Hence the nickname.

"Who took him out?" Vera said, rifling through the poor guy's jeans for a wallet. She wasn't as squeamish as Nico.

"Gina, you come back with me. I need a calming influence." I followed Uncle Vito's stout body back into the restaurant.

"Everything is bueno, bueno," he assured the diners. "We just dropped a pan back there."

I walked back to my seat smiling all the way. Big fake smile pasted on my face. Several diners beamed back at me, including a few clients. I nodded to Dr. Drake, who was just sitting down, and to his wife, who had been waiting for him. She grinned widely and flashed her right hand. Big hulking sapphire recently purchased. I nodded in fake appreciation. No, that's not right. I appreciated her business, truly. I just couldn't think beyond the butchered body at the back door.

I reached my chair, sat down and stared into my cold coffee. Who the hell had shot Wally the Wanker? And why leave him on Vito's doorstep?

Don't get involved, my fickle conscience warned me. *Your wedding is just two months off. Your fiancé Pete is a great guy who has no idea how involved you still are with 'the family'. Keep it cool, Gina Gallo.*

I should be calling the cops. But the cops don't like me much, especially Rick Spenser, another high school non-friend. I didn't think he'd appreciate a call from me. He might even get the impression I had something to do with the hit. So I decided not to interrupt his Monday night poker game.

Maybe ten minutes passed before Nico came out from the back room. He sat down at our little table.

"All taken care of," he whispered. "We can leave now."

Phew! The relief. I couldn't wait to get out of there to put some distance between me and the recently departed.

I picked up my purse and jacket from the back of the chair. Nico followed me out of the restaurant and over to my car in the back parking lot.

When we were all buckled in, I said, "Shall I drop you off at your place?"

"Uh, no, not yet, Gina. We have something else to do first."

I pulled onto James.

"And you have to promise not to scream."

I gritted my teeth. "What did you do, Nico?"

"I put the body in your trunk."

"WHAT??" I slammed on the brakes and pulled over. A guy in a big SUV honked his horn three times and gave me the finger as he passed.

"It was Aunt Vera's idea. She helped. But don't worry. We've already notified Uncle Vince. We're to take your car to the chop shop. The guys will get it all clean, they promised."

I slammed my palm on the steering wheel. Then I took three deep breaths.

I didn't need to ask how Nico got the trunk of the car open without my keys. Mark that down to a misspent youth.

"I wasn't going to get involved. I WASN'T GOING TO GET INVOLVED. And now I have a dead body in the truck of my car. Nico, I could kill you!"

"Don't be silly. There's no more room in the trunk. Would you mind letting me off home first? It's on the way."

When we got to his condo, I nearly pushed him out.

It was almost nine. I drove to the place I was supposed to go. (Don't ask—I can't tell you.) It was a little place behind a little place in a not so well-lit area. The guys at the chop shop stared as I emerged from the car. They had the good sense not to cat call.

Tony (my second cousin Tony—meaning I have more than one) nodded at me.

"Gina. How's things?" He was wiping his greasy hands on an even greasier towel.

"Same ole, same ole. You?"

"Good. The twins are growing. You should come round." Tony looks like a Tony. And his wife Maria is equally front-page Italian.

He nodded to the trunk. "The Wanker dude?"

I gestured with both arms. "Not my body. I had nothing to do with it."

"No probs. I'll call you when the car's ready."

It was really dark and I wanted to get out of there. But I had no wheels. And I didn't want to be seen at this place, so that meant no taxi.

I called Pete's cell phone. "Hey, can you come pick me up?"

"Where's your car?" Pete asked.

"What?"

"Where is your car?" Pete repeated precisely.

"Oh." I thought fast. "It needed a little work, so I took it in."

"Does this have anything to do with the takeout on James?"

I shrieked a bit. Or at least, that's what Tony said it sounded like.

"What do you know about a murder on James?" I hissed into the phone.

"I work for a newspaper, remember? I hear everything."

"Well, UN-hear it. And get the others to un-hear it too." Jeez. All I needed was reporters following me around, and cops following them.

I gave Pete the address.

"I'm still at work. Pick you up in twenty."

Before I could put my cell back in my purse, it started singing "Shut Up and Drive."

"Wally the Wanker got whacked?" It was Sammy the String Bean, Vince's right hand.

I hesitated. "Two plugs from a .38. You mean you didn't do it?" I wasn't going to say 'we'. There is no 'we' in my vocab when it comes to murder.

"No way, Sugar. This is interesting. Gotta go talk to Vince." He hung up.

Sure, it was. Interesting, that is.

I was still mulling it over when Pete drove up in his hot little convertible. I hopped in and didn't look back.

Next morning I called my cousin Paulo, the lawyer. He was my go-to guy for family gossip.

"What was Wally the Wanker into?" I asked.

"Officially—parking lots. He cruised the lots looking for vehicles that should be removed, if you get my drift. But unofficially—meaning without the family blessing—drugs. The upmarket kind. Peddled it to the nose bleed crowd."

I promised to take him out to lunch next week, and sat back to think.

Around noon, I phoned Sammy.

"How much do you want to know about what went down last night?" I said.

"I want to know. But I don't want the cops to know," said Sammy.

"So we keep it to ourselves. Gotcha. Meet me at La Paloma at five."

Nico and I got there at four thirty, before the doors opened. I had a few questions to ask the staff, specifically who had arrived in the restaurant before whom, the night before. Double check my memory, so to speak.

Sammy got there at five on the dot. He was alone.

Vera and Vito came out to the public area and we all took a seat around a table for six. All except me. I think better on my feet.

"You gonna tell us what happened, Gina? 'Cause I don't get it. Why dump a body here? It's a nice place." Vera wiped her hands on the apron spread across her ample lap.

I turned to Sammy. "We're keeping this between us, right? Not telling the cops, unless we have to? 'Cause I can't prove it, you know. It's just conjecture."

Sammy nodded. He's a wiry guy, about fifty, with Woody Allen hair; he's also sharp as a shark's tooth. I adore him.

"You go, girl."

I smiled and leaned forward, putting both hands on the white tablecloth. "Wally the Wanker was making a little extra on the side, peddling OxyContin to the upper classes. Nice work if you can get it. But then his source started to shut down. Wanted out of it. So Wally resorted to his high school trade—remember what that was, Nico?"

Nico shivered. "Blackmail."

All eyes swung to Nico.

"Sonamabeech." You could see Aunt Vera calculating what Nico had been in the frame for, back then.

"Got it in one," I said, straightening up. I talk with my hands a bit, so they need to be free.

"So. Wally started to blackmail the source because he wouldn't come through with the dope anymore. And the source didn't think that was nice. So he took out Wally with a .38." I flicked my arm to the side. "Doesn't matter where. Then he dumped the body on the back steps of La Paloma, that noted 'family' hangout, when no one was looking."

"I don't get it," said Vera.

"The killer hoped the takeout would be put down to us," Sammy said. His brown eyes were piercing.

I nodded.

"Well, that won't happen. We've taken care of it. No body, no crime. Nothing to report." Sammy sat back and folded his spindly arms. "I'll spread a rumour that Wally left The Hammer for his health. So all that remains is you naming the killer, Sugar."

This was the fun part. I grinned and pointed to the ring on my left hand.

"You know me. I notice jewelry—can't help it. And that sapphire ring was niggling at me." I paused for effect. "Doctors make a lot of money, but they don't make THAT much. Last night in this restaurant, Mrs. Drake was wearing the ring she bought from my store last month. You wanna talk money—that rock makes my twenty grand engagement ring look like a dollar store bauble. Then I remembered she entered the restaurant alone last night. Dr. Drake came in about five minutes later. That's because he was dumping the body out back. Then he drove around the front, parked, and pretended to just get here."

"But..." started Vera.

"What better way to score illicit Oxy than from a bona fide doctor." Sammy cursed. "Ah, Wally. You stupid bastard."

"He was a *blackmailer*, Sammy." Nico had his chin up and his arms crossed. "I know Wally's dead now, but I can't feel sorry for him. Even if he was employed by the family. "

"That's why we're not going to say a word about it," I said, pulling out a chair.

"No body, no crime. You see a body around here?" Sammy waved both his arms.

Sometime later, when we'd had our fill of veal Marsala and a real tasty Amarone, Nico said, "Peacocks, Gina. For the wedding. What do you think?"

I looked at Uncle Vito and winked. "Fine with me. Do you have a good recipe?"

Nico gasped. "You wouldn't! I meant—"

Aunt Vera got that one.

About Melodie Campbell

Melodie Campbell achieved a personal best in 2013 when Library Digest compared her to Janet Evanovich.

Melodie has a Commerce degree from Queen's University, but it didn't take well. She has been a bank manager, marketing director, college instructor, comedy writer, and possibly the worst runway model ever.

Melodie got her start writing comedy (stand-up and columns.) She was invited into the Toronto Press Club in 1994. In 1999, she opened the Canadian Humour Conference. She has over two hundred publications including one hundred comedy credits, forty short stories and four novels. Her fifth novel, a mob caper entitled *The Goddaughter's Revenge* (Orca Books), will be released October 1, 2013. She has won six awards for fiction, and was a finalist for both the 2012 Derringer and Arthur Ellis Awards.

Connect with Melodie at:
www.melodiecampbell.com
Facebook: Melodie Campbell Author
Twitter: @melodiecampbell
www.mesdamesofmayhem.com

The Emerald Skull

by Sylvia Maultash Warsh

I'm not one of those UFO freaks who think the U.S. government is hiding flying saucers in New Mexico. I don't believe in alternate universes or horoscopes. But I am an artist and an artist should keep an open mind. I nearly missed the story when I threw the newspaper on the floor to catch paint drips. Then the brilliant green caught my eye: an emerald skull held at arm's length by an old woman. She was gazing at it with staged awe. The headline read: *Does the Skull heal those who seek its powers?* I bent over to read the caption: "The emerald is the sacred stone of Venus, the goddess of love and beauty. It is thus thought to preserve love and heal the heart."

You wouldn't think I'd be someone who needed healing. Poor little rich girl, you'd say. But my mother abandoned me when I was two and once I was old enough to understand, I came to the only possible conclusion: if my own mother couldn't love me, I must be unlovable. My whole life I'd been looking to fill the hole in my heart sucked out by her leaving. Maybe an emerald skull could succeed where all else had failed.

I skimmed the interview with Eugenia Vanderhof, the woman who found the skull in Guatemala in 1958. She was eighteen when she accompanied her father on an archaeological expedition. In another photo, a group shot, muddy with age, the large ungainly girl held onto her father's arm, while on his other side, a slim pretty woman stood next to two men in shorts.

Hold on! The woman… It couldn't be! Through the murk of the photo, I swore I was looking at *myself.* A young version of myself, anyway, since I was no longer young. The caption read: Eugenia with Willem Vanderhof and crew. Crew!

I grabbed the magnifying glass I used when painting detail and aimed it at the photo: the black and white newsprint dots enlarged into confounding halftones. My double was slender and tanned with a curve of dark hair, like mine was thirty years ago; she was leaning into the tropical sun, turned slightly toward Vanderhof, as if he were the centre. Fit and dignified in white shirt and shorts, he faced the camera head on for posterity, a pipe held between aristocratic lips.

I read the interview more carefully then, to see if the mystery woman was identified. But Eugenia was interested only in herself. She went on about her miserable childhood—you'd think she could get past that, now that she was an old woman with white hair. It seemed she had suffered the kind of deprivation one expected of aristocracy: her mother had gone mad and been sent to an institution. I was reading between the lines, since she didn't actually admit it. But I recognized the obfuscation in words like "indisposed" and "didn't like company," and "was away a lot."

At least she *had* a mother. For a long time after mine disappeared, when anyone asked about her, Father trotted out his story: she had taken a prolonged trip abroad to find new scenery to paint. Since she was a gifted artist, people believed it at first. After a while they stopped asking. While

I was a child, I thought she would come home someday. When I was fifteen, Father sat me down and told me the truth. She had run away with an adventurer who would probably leave her in some godforsaken foreign country where she would fall prey to slave traders. Ha! The way he told it, she deserved that fate. Over the years he had become a bitter man, withered by his self-imposed loneliness. I felt like an orphan, raised by a series of nannies. Though I often wondered where she was, I was too angry to admit it, blaming her for my unhappiness. I googled her a few times but nothing ever came up. What kind of a person left behind her baby girl?

I stared at the photo in the paper. Was this Dorothea Beckwith? A pretentious name, but one etched in my heart. Father had thrown out all the pictures of her but one, which I had found at the back of his closet: their wedding photo, her face radiant with a smile. This woman's smile in the paper was not radiant—more tentative, the face you showed when the photographer said *Smile*, and you didn't feel like it. That's why it looked like me. I had never smiled the way my mother did in her wedding photo. It all fit. I would've been two in 1958. And Vanderhof by any definition was an adventurer.

How better to escape a difficult home life than to chase dreams around the globe. His life's aspiration was to find the lost continent of Atlantis. Well, I'd heard Atlantis had sunk to the bottom of the ocean millennia ago. But what did I know?

The photo had been reprinted from Eugenia's autobiography, *Fate Led Me*, published in 1970. The author would surely say what happened to her father—and more importantly, my mother.

I applied for the book in the basement of the reference library, pacing while the librarian fetched it. *Fate Led Me* was a disappointingly slim volume but I cradled it in my hand like a precious artifact. Sitting at a table, I flipped through the photos with an impatient hand. Then I found it. I held my breath. A tanned slender woman with a curve of dark hair one crew-member away from Willem Vanderhof. This time she was identified: *Dorothea Beckwith*. It was her! Marking the page with my fingertip, I searched for more.

Eugenia was a large girl caught by the camera holding onto her father's arm, squinting into the sun, hand on one hip. She had left school when she was sixteen to accompany him on his explorations. Apparently the charming Vanderhof was able to persuade rich fools to lay out large sums of money for these forays. She put it differently in the interview: "My father was a respected explorer and never had problems attracting financing." Looking for Atlantis couldn't have been cheap.

Dorothea Beckwith was sketching the quest to preserve it for posterity. No mention of her industrialist husband, Robert Beckwith—my father—or the heartbreak manufactured for him by the happy couple. Where had she met Willem? People with money found each other somehow.

Several plodding chapters about the difficult trip inland along a treacherous river to a village where natives took them further in dugout canoes. I wasn't interested in the stinging insects or the thorny vegetation or the river drying up, forcing them to get out and pull the boats over sandbanks. I flipped pages until my mother's name came up again. It seemed, one fine morning, Willem and Dorothea vanished. A dugout canoe was gone, as well as some of their clothing. No other information.

The chapter was curiously flat. There was no emotion in Eugenia's tone: she must've been badly hurt. We had that in common. I moved the magnifying glass over the pictures, trying to see more than what was there, to burrow beneath the surface of the dots for some flash of insight that would make it all come clear.

The paper had said Eugenia lived in Bradford, a small town north of Toronto. It was easy to find her address. She had a website from which you could order her book as well as crystals that had been "charged" by the skull, photos of the skull signed by Eugenia, photos of the expedition, and so on. You just had to send your cheque or money order to an address in Bradford. I'd let the maid go for the weekend, so I would have to drive myself. Father would not have approved, but he'd been dead three years now and I could do what I wanted.

It was surprisingly easy to jump into my BMW and head north up the 400 to Bradford, a farming town. There was no one to say goodbye to; I'd never married or had children. Father had taken up much of my time, requiring my presence after he retired. When he got sick in the end, he hated other people looking after him. I raced up the highway like a teenager, the music blaring. He would have been appalled. He was my one parent but I had never pleased him. As a child I had gravitated toward art, despite Father's concern that I was following in my mother's footsteps. That was the point. Painting brought me closer to her. I never knew what her subjects were—he had burned all her canvases—so I painted to please myself. Abstract watercolours in clashing purples and blues and greens that could have represented anything, but were always approximations of her. My trying to remember, but only channeling the anger she left in her wake. I didn't need the money, but developed a bit of a following with people as lost as me—who else would buy those pieces of my rage?

In less than an hour I was passing fields of green shoots in black earth that reminded me it was May. The old lady lived in a Victorian brick house set back on its own isolated cul-de-sac with no neighbours. I sat in the car, engine running. What was I going to say to her?

Finally, I walked up the worn wooden stairs to the house. The sweeping branches of a huge maple tree shaded the yard, making it cool and dark. I knocked. A lacy curtain hung over the glass of the door. No movement. I knocked harder. A light went on in the hall.

The door opened a crack and a female voice from inside said, "Healing sessions over for the year." The door slammed shut. The light went off.

I hadn't expected an English accent. I knocked again. "I want to buy a crystal."

The voice behind the door shouted, "Send a cheque in the mail!"

I shouted back, "I want to buy *lots of* crystals. I've got cash."

The light went back on. The door opened wide enough this time to reveal the woman inside, oddly imposing in black jogging pants and a pink golf shirt. She was taller than I expected, striking, with her white hair fluffed out like a cloud. Didn't people shrink when they got old?

Her eyes narrowed in the unaccustomed light, her mouth opened to utter something banal to the stranger at her door. But no words arrived. Her fleshy cheeks began to wobble. Her face paled at the sight of me and her hand flew up to her heart.

"No," she muttered, staggering. "Not yet. Please."

I stepped forward and put out my hand to help. To my surprise, the woman shrieked and reeled backwards.

"No!" she cried. "I'm not ready."

My heart sank. The woman was senile and thought I was Dorothea. I'm no longer young but I'm well-preserved for my age, still chestnut-haired and slim.

"There's nothing to be afraid of," I said. "I'm Lydia Beckwith, Dorothea's daughter."

Eugenia stopped cringing and stared harder. In a moment she straightened up, pulling back her shoulders.

"Oh," she murmured. "Oh. I forgot she *had* a daughter."

My chest started to ache with the old desolation. "I'm sorry I startled you," I said. The woman kept her hand over her heart, but had calmed down. "When did she die, then?" I asked.

The woman cocked her white head to one side. "I'm sure I don't know."

"But you know she *is* dead?"

"I know nothing of the kind."

She glared at me as if I were an idiot. This would not be easy.

"When was the last time you saw her?" I knew what the book said, but wanted to hear it from her own lips.

Eugenia shook her head, dismissing the question. "Not since I was a young girl."

I tried a different tack. "Well, when did you last hear from your father?"

Eugenia's small vacant eyes looked away, down the street. Anywhere. "They left in 1958. I never saw either of them again."

"Surely they wrote you from where they went," I said, losing patience. "It's all right. You can tell me. There's nothing anyone can do to hurt them now."

Eugenia shook her head slowly. "I told you..." Then she saw something in the distance, a squirrel, a falling leaf, an idea. "They sent me a postcard a few years later. From Australia."

I couldn't tell if the old woman was confused, or trying to confuse *me*.

"Your father... my mother... they left us," I said, trying to find a common bond. "We were both left behind." I finally had her attention. "Would you mind if I..." I motioned inside the house. "I just want to talk."

Eugenia watched me from beneath heavy lids. "You aren't here for the crystals, are you?"

"I'll buy some crystals. If we can talk."

Reluctantly, she let me in.

As I followed her down the hallway, my throat began to close up. There was no *air*, as if the windows had been shut for years. She startled me, leaping ahead to pull closed a green velvet curtain to the dining room. Then she gestured me into the parlour with an impatient hand. The little light from the shaded window did not clarify, but blurred the edges of the busy room. It was like stepping into 1950—both the furnishings, and the musty absence of air. A large stuffed peacock languished on the Persian rug, its iridescent tail feathers trailing between two ornate pink velvet chairs. Their mahogany arms terminated in the carved heads of stately women, their bosoms curving into chair legs.

I placed my feet carefully, so as not to step on the tail feathers. There was an awkward silence. "You have a lovely large property," I said. "No neighbours."

"That's the way I like it."

"Could I have something to drink?" I said.

She observed me like a bug she had just spotted on the carpet.

"You could show me some crystals while we have tea."

Peevishly, she stomped into the kitchen where I could hear her filling a kettle and clattering some china.

I approached the dining room and creaked open one of the French doors a crack. My jaw dropped. The emerald skull grinned up at me from a black velvet cloth on the dining room table. Its radiant green dome and eye sockets had absorbed every speck of light in the dim air. Votive candles flickered on either side, and, arranged in a semi-circle around the skull, were photos of Willem Vanderhof. My heart shrank.

As I stepped toward the shrine, the conical eye sockets of the skull shifted green light. The nose was an oval crater above perfect teeth. I put my hand out to touch the lustrous pate and was startled to see my fingers, shrunk to green miniature, shining in the eye sockets. The crystal forehead was shockingly smooth, almost vulnerable. The photos of Vanderhof were flattering shots, ranging from youth to middle-age, all with the ubiquitous pipe lodged in the corner of his mouth. A handsome lanky man, tanned from the sun.

"Get out of there!" Eugenia snapped behind me, holding a tray. "You have no right."

"I didn't mean to intrude." I needed to distract her. "I couldn't help myself—it's so beautiful."

"Not 'it.' *He.*"

"I so envy you, having him here. Do you know who made it? I mean 'him?'" I blinked to convey innocent curiosity.

She glared at me, yet my groveling must have mollified her.

Grudgingly she put the tray down on a side table. "Some experts say it's impossible he was made on earth.

But my father said it was the advanced civilization in Atlantis."

I nodded expectantly, hoping she would keep talking. I didn't want to leave.

"The Knights Templar thought he was holy and carried him around during the crusades."

"May I... touch him?"

"He doesn't like anyone touching him but me."

She made me walk ahead as she carried the tray to the living room where we sat down.

Lodged in one of the ornate chairs, she was about to open a black velvet bag, presumably filled with crystals, when I said, "I read your book." I sat on a floral sofa sipping tea from a china cup. "I found it"—I recalled the plodding prose, the long parts I skipped—"fascinating." I *had*, but for my own reasons.

"Why, thank you," Eugenia said, smiling for the first time. "Then you know my whole story."

I returned the smile. "I loved the part where you found... him. That must've been an emotional day."

"It was fate that brought me to him, I'm sure. I think of that day often. We'd been digging in the area for weeks. I can take myself back there anytime, just close my eyes and there I am at the foot of that old pyramid. Everyone asleep, early in the morning. Just me and the sounds of the jungle. I was slashing around with my machete—you couldn't go two steps without clearing the jungle vegetation. And I almost stepped right on him. You should've seen the green glow of him buried in the vines. It was a signal. He shone right in my eyes. He *wanted* me to find him. I knew he was special as soon as I touched him."

Eugenia sat back, satisfied with her account of events.

"Where was my mother then?"

Eugenia's smile dissolved. "How should *I* know?"

"Would you mind," I said softly, "telling me a bit about her?"

Eugenia sighed in the chair with the carved heads. "I'm sure I couldn't tell you anything you don't already know."

"Well, you see I was very young when... when she left. I was only two. I don't remember her at all."

Why had I expected any sympathy from Eugenia? Her small dull eyes watched me without emotion. "I wrote everything I knew in the book."

There had been remarkably little said about Dorothea in the book, barely enough to make sense of what happened in the end.

"Did your father know Dorothea before the expedition?"

"Yes, of course."

So, my mother had gone off in the full knowledge that she might not return. Or maybe it had been an impulsive decision, love in the middle of the rainforest, exotic birds flashing colours among lush vines.

"Was she beautiful?" I asked.

"Some thought so."

The implication being that Eugenia didn't. "You don't blame her... "

"She *was* to blame."

"He was a grown man."

"She bewitched him!"

The hatred in her voice took me aback. Maybe *he* bewitched *her*. Maybe my mother had actually loved me. But I was not going to engage this crazy woman in dialogue that could only end in angry words.

"When did you first know they were gone?"

"It's in the book."

"I've forgotten."

Eugenia pursed her lips in displeasure. "Their clothes were gone. And there was a note."

The book had said only some of their clothes were gone; there was no mention of a note.

"What did the note say?"

"Well, what *could* it say? I can't remember after all these years. They were gone, that's what it said. To Australia."

I fingered my teaspoon—I didn't believe her. If *I* had found such a note, the words would have engraved themselves on my heart.

"You make very good tea," I said, depositing my English china cup into its saucer. "It's Darjeeling, isn't it? I'd love another cup."

Eugenia stood with resignation. She gathered up the tray and headed into the kitchen.

Thank heaven for polite ritual, I thought. Even in madness, a hostess knew when to offer a guest more tea.

I jumped back toward the French door and stepped in once more. I didn't know what drew me there. The perfect dome of the skull? I could transform it into one of my angry paintings. The green would work in my colour scheme. I imagined light and more light repeating endlessly in the translucent brain. But it wasn't the skull. I turned to Willem's photos. Strangely they roused no animosity in me, merely sadness. Then I noticed the two small drawers that hung beneath the table.

Eugenia was still shuffling about in the kitchen. I pulled open the first drawer. A small booklet with a cardboard cover lay among old photos of Vanderhof in explorer mode. I turned it over and saw it was a passport. Inside, a picture of Vanderhof in middle age—the document expired in 1959. An explosion went off in my head. He wouldn't have left his passport. He would've needed it to get anywhere.

My head began to swim with misgivings. I reached for the second drawer. A matching booklet, this time accompanied by a small tablet of watercolours. Sketches of jungle and natives and artifacts with the initials DB in the corner. And beneath them, some photos. Baby pictures. I stared at them, stupefied. Baby Lydia in her bonnet, Baby Lydia in a smart frilly dress, Baby Lydia in her mother's arms, Dorothea beaming like a proud young matron. She looked so happy. Written on the back of one photo: *Lydia and Mommy, June, 1957*.

My heart fluttered with the strangest mixture of joy and fear. I lifted the cardboard booklet from the drawer, fingers slow, uncertain. There she was, Dorothea Beckwith, her chestnut hair in sleek waves, looking back at me from the passport photo, unsmiling. My head swam. There was something to be said for certainty, even a painful one. My mother had abandoned me—*that* had been the certainty most of my life. I heard a sudden gasp behind me.

"They never went anywhere, did they?" I said.

"You know, he called it 'The Skull of Destiny,'" Eugenia said, her voice hoarse. "But he didn't understand."

She seemed to wait. I said, "What do you mean?"

"I wrote about it in my book."

"It must've been one of the parts I skipped."

In a low voice I could barely hear, she said, "The Maya had a ceremony with the skull called 'Gift of Death.' A deep and beautiful thing. An old person and a young child held onto the skull together while the priest chanted secret words. They drank a special potion. The child absorbed all the knowledge and wisdom of the older one through the medium of the skull. Then the old person was empty and died.

"Father wanted to take the skull away from me. I knew that was wrong. *I* found him and he belonged to me. And ever since, the skull has watched over me. He protects me. I feel quite safe with him in the house. Father understands that now."

I was dumbfounded. What had she done? "What about Dorothea? What happened to her?"

"I never understood what they talked about, her forever going on about her precious baby and how many words it knew already. I wanted to shake him for listening to her."

Her baby! Her precious baby! That was *me*. The pain in my heart didn't shrink, but shifted, changed direction. All those years of recrimination and self-loathing, all that time wasted when I should've been mourning.

"How did you kill them?"

Eugenia's eyes grew wide. "It was the skull, he has powers..."

He. It was the skull I had to thank for my suffering. Because Eugenia would not part from it. Because Eugenia was as mad as her mother. I imagined her finding them asleep together in his tent, then surprising herself and bringing down the terrible weight of the skull on their heads.

"What did you do with their bodies?"

Eugenia's eyes watched but didn't see. "Someone who hasn't been in the jungle wouldn't understand—the vegetation never stops, it just keeps growing and twisting around everything. Once a vine gets hold of you..."

I imagined my mother's bones braided with leaves. Long gone now, claimed by the jungle. The unfairness of it all! She would never have left me. She loved me! My head swam with images of the jungle. Or was it the room swimming? I closed my eyes. The truth was exhausting.

"You killed my mother," I mumbled. Why couldn't I speak clearly?

"He protects me," she said.

"From what?"

"Evil people."

"Am *I* evil?" I shook my head to get rid of the torpor.

It didn't work. The torpor sank into my feet. Then terror overtook me. Eugenia must've been in her seventies. But she was bigger than me, nearly six feet, and probably outweighed me by fifty pounds.

"You've put something in my tea," I murmured. I remembered the special potion in the Mayan 'Gift of Death.'

"It's for the best. Now move away."

She stepped closer, trying to approach the skull. I knew I would only get weaker. The poison would flow deep through my veins. While I still could, I turned to the table and picked up the skull with both hands. My skin reflected green.

"Don't touch him!" Her face twisted with outrage. "He's mine!"

She threw out her hands to snatch the skull from me. But a new energy, the unexpected power of a mother's love, coursed through my body. I found the strength from some hidden cave of myself to thrust the skull hard at her chest.

As she clutched it to her with both hands, she lost her balance. Lurching back, she fell heavy and hard. On her way down, her head smashed against the carved Amazon head of the chair-arm. She lay on her back, quite still, the white hair arranged around her head like a cloud. A worm of blood crept onto the carpet. I slid to the floor, spent.

Though the spring sun shone outside, the shade of the maple reached over the yard, shrouding the room.

I would never leave this house. She had no neighbours; no one would be coming to check on her. Our bodies would decompose on the carpet together. No jungle vines to grow over and reclaim us.

I crawled to the corner where the emerald skull had fallen. I could see why she was obsessed with it. The bit of light from the window radiated through it, expanding, contracting, dancing through the mirrors of its eyes. And inside one of the tiny mirrors, I saw her. My mother held out her hands to me from the jungle, riotous with green. Not an angry green. A green filled with love, like her eyes.

About Sylvia Maultash Warsh

Sylvia Maultash Warsh was born in Germany and came to Canada when she was four. She earned a BA and a Masters in Linguistics from the University of Toronto. Her short stories and poetry have appeared in Canada and the US.

Sylvia is the author of the Rebecca Temple mystery series published by Dundurn. *To Die in Spring*, 2000, was nominated for an Ellis Award for Best First Novel. *Find Me Again*, 2003, won an Edgar award from Mystery Writers of America and was nominated for two Anthonys. *Season of Iron*, 2006, was short-listed for a ReLit Award. *The Queen of Unforgetting*, published in 2010, was chosen for a plaque by Project Bookmark Canada. *Best Girl*, a Rapid Reads book, came out in 2012.

Sylvia lives in Toronto where she teaches writing to seniors.

Connect with Sylvia at:
www.sylviawarsh.com
Amazon.com
www.mesdamesofmayhem.com

The Sweetheart Scamster

by Rosemary McCracken

"Mrs. Sullivan is here for her appointment," Rose Sisto, my administrative assistant, announced at my office door.

I looked up from the papers I was studying as Trudy Sullivan slipped into the chair across from my desk. "Good morning, Pat," she said.

I smiled at my client. Trudy's silver hair had been cut in an attractive new style. She was wearing more makeup than usual, and it accentuated her high cheekbones and deep blue eyes. And she was sporting a smart fall suit. New hairdo, new makeup, new clothes. She looked fabulous— and far younger than her seventy-four years.

"A new man in your life, Trudy?" But as soon as the words were out of my mouth, I wanted to bite them back. Trudy had been mourning her husband's death for the past three years. I wasn't sure how she'd take my flip question.

"As a matter of fact there is. I'm seeing a nice gentleman."

She looked down at her hands for a moment. "Last week I took the last of Ernie's clothes to the Goodwill store. Yesterday I threw out his medication. I still miss him, but I need to get on with my life."

I realized then how lonely Trudy had been. She was Ernie's second wife, and from what he'd told me, they'd had a happy marriage. She became my client after his accident, and I'd been meeting with her every four months. She was a reserved woman, not given to joining clubs and social groups, and I had the impression that she had few friends. Her two daughters lived in other cities, and Ernie's sons seemed to have dropped her after their father's death. Yes, she had been lonely, but now she had someone in her life.

And that made me sit up straight in my chair. As a financial advisor, I'm well aware there are complexities to grey romance that are seldom present in youthful relationships. Ernie had been a heavy gambler, so Trudy had to be careful with her money. But she had his big home in Toronto's Beaches neighbourhood and enough investment income to stay there as long as her good health continued. I wanted to know more about this friend of hers. A lonely woman can be an easy mark for fortune hunters.

"What's your gentleman's name?" I asked.

"Jim." She didn't give his surname.

"I take it Jim's retired."

"Oh, yes."

"You see him on weekends? Saturday night dates?"

"Not just on weekends." She lowered her eyes again. "You might say we've become very close."

This romance had got off to a galloping start.

"We're not living together," she said, "but who knows...?"

I needed to ask some hard questions about Jim. What he did during his working years, where he lived, if he had a family. But I wasn't sure how to begin.

"Let's go over your investment portfolio." I hoped an opening would present itself there.

My mind was clicking away as I showed her the changes I'd made to her investments and explained why.

"Does Jim work with a financial advisor?" I asked when I'd finished.

"I don't know. He's never brought it up and I've never asked him."

Of course not. Trudy's generation of women consider it crass to talk about money.

Then she surprised me by asking for some.

"I need a bit extra this month, Pat. Ten thousand dollars."

Ten thousand dollars! I was about to launch into my spiel about living within her budget, but she beat me to it.

"You're going to say I mustn't run through my money if I want to stay in the house. Well, I may sell it."

I nearly fell off my chair. Trudy had been adamant about remaining in her home even though she would have had more money to live on if she'd downsized. Was Jim pressuring her to sell the house?

"It's something I'm considering," she continued, "but for now I need ten thousand dollars. Cash me out of some bonds."

It was her money, of course, but I wanted to know why she needed it. "You're planning something nice?" I asked.

She looked me in the eye. "A surprise for Jim."

I swallowed hard, and thought of contacting her daughters. But I quickly dismissed that idea. It would be a breach of client confidentiality.

I looked at the woman seated across from me. Trudy was a competent adult with every right to form a new relationship and do whatever she wanted with her money.

I told her the ten grand would be in her bank account in a few days. But I had grave misgivings as I watched her leave my office.

"You look worried," my business partner Stéphane Pratt said when he sat down in the client's chair five minutes later.

I told him about Trudy's new beau, and that she planned to surprise him with a lavish gift.

"You think he's one of those sweetheart scamsters?" Stéphane asked.

"Is that what they're called?"

"I watched a television program on sweetheart fraud," he said. "The scamster tries to win the affection of a lonely person, then takes over his or her financial affairs. When the money is gone, the sweetheart leaves the victim."

"Trudy was very astute when we went over Ernie's financial statements, and now she wants updates on all her holdings. I can't see her falling prey to one of those crooks." But I couldn't shake the idea she'd been taken in by a con man who would leave her destitute and heartbroken.

Stéphane gave me a tight smile. "When people fall in love, common sense flies out the window."

A week later, Trudy reached me on my cell phone. As soon as I heard her voice, I braced myself for a request for more money.

"I thought I'd let you know Jim and I are getting married," she said. "I'm changing my will. My lawyer will send you a copy."

"Married!" Then I remembered my manners. "I wish you every happiness, Trudy. When's the big day?"

"Friday."

"This Friday?"

"We're not getting any younger, so there's no point in waiting. We'll go down to city hall with Jim's friend Kenneth and his wife. After the ceremony, we'll all go out for lunch."

"The girls won't be at your wedding?"

"We thought we'd surprise Beth and Mary Lou afterwards."

Red flags went up in my mind. It sounded like Jim was pressuring her into a hasty marriage. Not giving her time for second thoughts. And by not telling her daughters until after the wedding, they couldn't talk her out of it.

I was about to ask whether she and Jim had drawn up a marriage contract, but she told me she was off to visit her hairdresser and hung up.

Once again, I thought of contacting her daughters, but my professional ethics prevented me. And there was a possibility I was mistaken. I'd never met Jim. He might be just the man to brighten Trudy's golden years.

Then I thought of the will she was changing. Had that been her idea—or Jim's? And what were the changes?

After work that day, I dropped by Trudy's home with a bottle of champagne. The *For Sale* sign on the front lawn put me into full alert.

If Trudy was surprised to see me, she didn't show it. She was perfectly turned out in a plum-coloured dress and a pearl necklace. As I handed her the champagne, a white-haired man hobbled into the hall with the help of a cane.

"My fiancé, Jim," Trudy said. "Honey, this is Pat Tierney, my financial advisor."

She took my coat, and Jim led me into the living room, where he poured glasses of sherry. He handed me a glass, and clinked his against Trudy's.

I raised my glass to them. "To the happy couple. May you have years of health and happiness together, although I see it won't be here. You're selling the house."

"Yes," Trudy said. "We're looking at condos downtown."

I wondered if Jim had a home of his own to sell, but I decided this was a social call. I'd arrange a meeting with Trudy after the wedding to go over the financial implications of her new situation. I'd suggest that Jim attend as well.

But there was one question I couldn't resist asking. "Do you have a family, Mr....?"

"Call me Jim," he said with a twinkle in his eyes. "No family, unfortunately. My late wife Rita and I weren't blessed with children."

I settled into an armchair with my sherry. They took seats on the sofa across from me.

"How did you two meet?" I asked.

"On an Alaskan cruise in June." Trudy held up a hand. "Don't worry, Pat. It didn't cost me a penny. Beth and her husband Steve wanted me to see my new grandson. They paid for my flight to Vancouver, and I stayed with them a week. Then they put me on the cruise."

Jim took her hand and looked at me. "We were seated at the same table at the captain's dinner. We chatted, found we had common interests. I don't think either of us realized until then how lonely we were, Trudy without Ernie and me without Rita. We began to see each other when we got back to Toronto, and...well, here we are." He gave Trudy a peck on the cheek.

I pasted a smile on my face, and they told me about their wedding plans. Trudy said she'd made a reservation for a late lunch at La Madeleine, an upscale restaurant in trendy Yorkville. And they would spend the weekend at the

Four Seasons Hotel down the street. They seemed to be looking forward to their life together.

I tried to find out more about their living arrangements. "When will you move downtown?"

"We'll stay here until the house sells," Trudy said.

Jim tapped his left hip with his cane. "I avoid stairs whenever I can, so a home without them makes sense. Fortunately, this house has a main-floor bedroom with an ensuite."

"Why not stay here?" I asked.

"We thought we should make a fresh start," Trudy said. "In a home of our own."

It sounded like the sale of her house would finance their condo. With money left over for two to live on.

She gave Jim a sunny smile. "Honey, I have a surprise for you." She glanced at me. "I've booked us on a cruise for our honeymoon. A ten-day Mediterranean vacation."

So that was what she'd wanted the money for. The cruise seemed to be her idea, but I wondered whether Jim had planted it in her mind.

"Sweetheart." He took both her hands in his and chuckled. "And I thought you had your heart set on Niagara Falls."

I could see the lovebirds wanted to be on their own, so I finished my sherry and wished them happiness again.

"I'll see you to your car," Trudy said.

Outside the house, she turned to look at me. "Well?" Her blue eyes were shining.

"I think he's landed quite a catch." I paused. "There are financial implications to marriage, Trudy. Jim will own half your home."

She put a hand on my arm. "Don't worry. I know what I'm doing."

She gave me a little wave as I drove off.

Jim was affable and charming, I mused on the way home. But was he too charming? And did he really need that cane? I still knew nothing about the man my client would marry in a few days.

The next week, I received a copy of Trudy's will. She had made Jim her sole beneficiary, and her daughters weren't even mentioned. I learned Jim's full name, however. James Reynolds. Why did that sound familiar?

I needed to talk to Trudy about her will. Her daughters would be hurt when they learned she hadn't even left them her jewelry. I wrote a note on my calendar to call her in two weeks. I figured she'd be back from her honeymoon by then.

The following Monday, Stéphane blew into the office suite just before ten. *"Bonjour, ma chère."* He placed a Starbucks latte on my desk and a copy of *The Toronto World*. He pointed to the front page of the newspaper. "Take a look."

He had circled an article in blue ink. "Wealthy industrialist James Reynolds dead at 78," the headline read.

> James Reynolds, founder and former chief executive of The Reynolds Group, which dominated Canada's automotive sector in the 1970s and 1980s, died this weekend on a honeymoon cruise off the coast of Spain.
>
> Early Sunday morning, Mr. Reynolds was found crumpled at the foot of a staircase on the deck of Robertson Cruises' Princess Maria. His wife, the former Gertrude Sullivan, said he had stumbled coming down the stairs. According to

her statement to Spanish police, she called for help when she was unable to revive him.

The couple married in Toronto nine days before the accident.

I thought of Ernie's accident three years before. He and Trudy had been on holiday in Greece when he stumbled on a footpath along the top of a cliff and fell to his death below.

I looked up at Stéphane. "My God! It was Trudy who wanted to tie the knot quickly so Jim wouldn't have time for second thoughts. She must have slipped him some of Ernie's medication."

Stéphane looked puzzled.

"She gave him just enough to disorient him and cause him to fall—or be pushed—down that staircase. Jim told me he avoided stairs.

"I thought she was lonely after Ernie died," I went on. "But being alone doesn't necessarily mean being lonely."

A few days later, I received a letter from Trudy's lawyer saying she was transferring her account to another investment firm. I thought of going to the police, but what could I tell them? That she'd married a wealthy man who had died soon after the wedding. That two of her husbands had died in falls.

I thought of her last words to me. *I know what I'm doing.*

She certainly did.

About Rosemary McCracken

Born and raised in Montreal, Rosemary McCracken has worked on newspapers across Canada as a reporter, arts writer and reviewer, and editor.

She is now a Toronto-based freelance journalist, specializing in personal finance and the financial service industry.

Rosemary's short fiction has been published by Room of One's Own Press, Kaleidoscope Books and Sisters in Crime Canada.

Her mystery novel, *Safe Harbor*, was shortlisted for Britain's Crime Writers' Association's Debut Dagger Award in 2010. It was released as a paperback and an e-book by Imajin Books in 2012.

Black Water, the second Pat Tierney mystery, has just been released.

Connect with Rosemary at:
www.rosemarymccracken.com
BlogSite: rosemarymccracken.wordpress.com
FaceBook: Rosemary McCracken
Twitter: @RCMcCracken
www.mesdamesofmayhem.com

Sore Feet and Gold Dust:

A story of the Klondike

by Vicki Delany

My feet hurt.

My boots don't fit too well, and my feet always hurt at this time of night.

Six a.m. The musicians are packing up their instruments and the men are being shown the door. Sometimes there's trouble: a drunk wants to keep on dancing or shouts for the band to keep playing, but it's not often it's anything bad enough to bother us. The bouncers here are good, and the regular customers know the rules and don't want any stranger messing up things for everyone.

Mrs. MacGillivray, co-owner of the Savoy Saloon and Dance Hall, smiles at a big spender. I wonder how she keeps that smile on her face, with her ear turned just so towards the man and her chin pointed forward in rapt attention. He's almost melting under her charm. Here it comes: he's asking her if she'd like to get a bite of supper. Then he laughs, blushing and pulling at his tattered collar, telling her he'd say breakfast except that sounds so improper. She lets the smile fade slightly and her face fills with regret. "No, thank you," she says. No excuses, no 'perhaps another time.' Just no. He hasn't even noticed that her eyes never stop moving around the room, checking out the bartenders closing down, watching the girls for signs of illicit drinking, observing the men, looking for anyone who might be in the mood to cause problems.

She flutters her eyelashes, waves the tips of her fingers, and the stranger leaves, dejected and disappointed.

She turns towards us, the group of girls standing by the bar watching her, jerks her head, and heads for the stairs.

Time to hand in our drink chips and, thank God, get paid and go home and off these aching feet.

At six in the morning, the town of Dawson, Yukon, is a mighty strange place. The streets are full with purposeful people going to work, starting their day—and those who can barely remain upright, staggering back to their lodgings. Some, who can't remain upright, are sleeping it off in doorways or even smack dab in the middle of the street. If they're lucky, they'll get a kick in the ribs from a Mountie before a horse and wagon comes along.

A man steps out of the shadows. My heart leaps into my throat and I step backwards, almost falling off the duckboard into the muck of the street. This is a peaceful town, a lot safer than most, but still...

"Beg pardon, Ma'am," he says, touching the brim of his hat, "I didn't mean to startle you."

"You didn't," says I, trying to retain some pride, although my pride isn't worth much, let me tell you.

"I enjoyed our dance very much and was hoping I could invite you to tea later today."

He takes a step into the weak morning light and I recognize him. I danced a couple of times with him earlier. That's my job at the Savoy. I'm a percentage girl. I come in at midnight when the stage show ends and dance with the men until six—dollar a dance, which includes a drink. I'd love to be a stage performer. They make lots more money than us, and they don't have to stay after the show to be pawed over by drunken miners trying to forget about the failure of their dreams in one fast-moving minute. It don't matter that I don't have the looks—some of the girls in the back row could play the part of horses if the show required it—or that I'm not small and dainty. Not many small and dainty women make it over the Chilkoot trail carrying two thousand pounds of goods on their back. No, it's just that Mrs. MacGillivray scarcely notices me. I tried to talk to her once to ask if I could replace that girl in the back who'd broken her ankle—pretty careless the way she let herself get bumped off the stage—but some drunk threw up on the floor and she was off in a right rage. When she hands me my night's wages, there's always a line of girls behind me, and every one of 'em wants to get home as fast as I do, and wouldn't thank me for holding things up.

The man speaks well, I notice that right away. His clothes ain't rags either, and he doesn't smell bad. A line of rough stitching holds his collar together, and his white shirt's grimy around the cuffs. I figure he don't have a wife, not one up here at any rate, to keep him stitched and pressed. But he's a darn sight more presentable than a lot of men in the Yukon. His fingernails are clean—that's a rarity—and a thick gold ring circles the little finger of his right hand. The rising sun flashes on a gold chain disappearing into his waistcoat.

He's not young, about sixty maybe. He gives me a nice smile and I can see he has most of his teeth.

"Tea, how lovely," I says, trying to sound like Mrs. MacGillivray. I've been practising talking like she does, which ain't easy for a Ukrainian farm girl from Manitoba.

The man falls in step beside me and we begin to walk. Across the street I see a couple of the dancers watching us. One of them nudges her companion and points towards me and they laugh. Stuck up cows. I let my new gentleman friend slip his arm though mine. The morning sun's warm, but there's a solid bite to the wind, telling us winter's coming fast.

"Four o'clock?" he says. "The Richmond Hotel?"

"Sure. I mean, yes that would be most delightfully lovely."

He doesn't release my arm and we round the corner into King Street. Once we're out of sight of the dancers, I pull my arm away. "See you at four," I says.

"May I escort you home?"

As if I don't know what that means. I'm having none of that. Mrs. MacGillivray fired a girl for using the dance hall to troll for after-hours customers, if you get my meaning. Besides, at this time of the morning, my bed ain't usually empty.

"No," I say, "I mean, no thank you, Mr., uh..."

"Jones, Albert Jones is my name."

"I'm Sarah Richards."

"I know."

He touches the brim of his hat, ever such a gentlemanly gesture, and walks away.

And that's the end of that, I think. His offer of tea's nothing but an excuse to walk with me and invite himself back to my room. Once I told him that weren't on, I don't expect I'll ever see him again.

I sigh and go home.

Home is one room in a broken-down boarding house on Fourth Street. A cheap room barely big enough for a bed and table, a row of hooks on the wall to hang clothes from, and a privy out back. The bed's small, the mattress thin and stained, the sheets threadbare and the blanket patched many times. The whole house smells of vomit, sweat, stale liquor and dead dreams.

I have to wait outside the privy, almost dancing in my need to be inside. I think about the ring on my 'admirer's' finger and the gold watch chain. I've never had a proper tea, like I hear they serve at the Richmond, with sandwiches and little cakes.

Finally I can do my business. In my room, I hang my dress on the hook, wash as best I can in the remains of the cold dirty water in the basin on the table, and approach the bed. Fortunately it's warm enough still that I can sleep in my shift and the blanket's not necessary. How I'll manage come winter, I can't imagine.

I shove at the lump in the bed. It don't move, so I shove again. He groans and rolls over. A foul stench fills the room, so bad I almost gag.

I crawl into bed, and try to sleep in the few inches of bed my sprawling husband's left for me.

I wake up to see the sun high in the sky and light pouring in through the threadbare curtains. The bed's empty and I stretch out in the middle of it, luxuriating in the space. I dreamed I was back at the farm, and my ma was tearing a strip off me for letting my dress get so filthy. I'd give almost anything to be back at the farm. I wouldn't even mind Pa tanning my hide for daydreaming and not noticing the milk spilling over the pail.

I open my eyes. Joshua's hand's in the pocket of my dress. I swear under my breath and he looks over at me.

"Mornin' darlin'" he says, with a flash of a smile and good white teeth. That smile charmed the knickers off me once. It don't no more.

My fool head was so full of dreams of tea and sandwiches last night I forgot to hide some of my wages.

"I need that money," I says. "We're almost out of bacon."

He puts a coin on the table.

"That's not enough. My boots ain't no good for dancing all night, and the bottom's about to come out of one of 'em. I need to buy new shoes."

He eyes the money and carefully adds a dollar bill.

"That ain't enough," I says.

"Not much longer, Sarah my darlin', and you'll have so many shoes you'll be changing three times a day to use them all."

There's never any point in arguing with him. He don't care enough to argue back. All I can do is roll my eyes towards the large, spreading, wet spot on the ceiling. One day the whole place is gonna come down on top of us.

He puts the rest of my money in his pocket before sitting on the edge of the bed. He reaches for me, but I swat his arm away. "I need more than that for new shoes."

"It'll have to do, Sarah. I've almost enough to buy that claim. A couple more weeks wearing old boots and eating beans and bacon will be worth it when the gold starts coming in, won't it?"

He leans forward to kiss me, but I turn my head away. Joshua and his gold mine. I doubt there's any claim, and if there is, he's being suckered into buying it. I rarely smell drink on him, and there ain't signs of another woman, but he's spending almost every penny of my earnings, and not bringing in nothing I can see in the way of wages of his own.

Joshua runs his finger down the side of my face, barely touching the skin. "Have faith, darlin'," he says. Then he gets up and, with a wink, he leaves.

Faith. I stopped believing in Joshua and his dreams a long time ago.

Judging by the sun, it's shortly after three. It's unlikely Mr. Jones will be at the Richmond, waiting for me as if I were a lady or something.

But right now, I need something to believe in.

I'm early and don't want to look too eager. Just in case he shows up, I duck into a dry goods shop and look over the merchandise as if I'm considering buying something. The woman behind the counter gives me a look that would freeze the Yukon River in July. I feel my face flush. I'm about to leave when a couple of sturdy women in homespun dresses come in and she hurries over to attend to them.

Joshua. He was a drifter, wandering into town in the fall, hired on by my pa to help with the harvest. Pa asked Joshua to stay on for the winter when one of the regular men fell through a rotten floorboard in the top of the bunkhouse in September and broke both his legs. He shouldn't have been trying for a kiss, should he?

Joshua was handsome and smart, and he'd been to Toronto. He was eighteen and I was fifteen. He told me I was beautiful and said he'd take me to Toronto one day. He made me pregnant in the hayloft while a snowstorm blew across the prairie.

He went to my parents and said he'd marry me, but my mother said she weren't going to let no child of hers marry a damn Protestant, and my father said I was a whore and he never wanted to see me again. We left the farm that day, and we've never been back.

I was five months along when the baby died. Just as well, really. What kind of life could we give it?

We were in Seattle on our way to California—we were always on our way somewhere—when news of the strike in the Klondike hit town. Well, from then on Joshua would hear nothing but that we were off to find gold to make ourselves rich. He had some money then. I don't know where it came from; he said an uncle had died. Joshua said a lot of things. It was enough to pay for our passage to Skagway and the goods we needed to get into Canada. He bought mining equipment, shiny new stuff. I carried those axes and pans and shovels over the pass on my own back. When we got to Dawson, Joshua decided mighty quick that working a mine for someone else weren't for him, and he sold it all for pennies on the dollar. He said there was more money to be made as a businessman or mine owner than a common labourer. He was right about that. Look at Mrs. MacGillivray with her jewels and fancy dresses. Look at the cow who owns this shop. But Joshua ain't no businessman. He's too ready to believe anyone that tells him what he wants to hear.

He went up to the Creeks, to see what's what, he said, and came back all puffed up about some claim he's wanting to buy. Ha. I told him everyone says all the good claims are taken, but he says this one only looks like it's empty. There's a secret vein the current owner hasn't found, so it's going cheap. He just needs a bit more money and he can buy it.

The only money I see coming in is what I make at the Savoy. He says he put the money he got from selling our things into the bank. Least he don't seem to spend any more on himself than he does on me.

The boarding house where we live is so cheaply made there are cracks in the walls and loose floorboards. I made a little hidey-hole in the wall behind where I hang my dresses, big enough to fit a small tobacco tin. There I put some of my wages every day. Unless, like last night, I forget. He hasn't found it yet. When there's enough for a steamship ticket out of here, I'll be leaving. I walked in—I sure ain't walking out.

I'll go to Manitoba and the farm and beg them to take me back. Eating crow's better than eating nothing at all.

I'm thinking of the farm and the way the land is so flat you can see forever, unlike here where there are hills and mountains all around, choking a person, closing you in, when Mr. Jones walks past the shop window.

I'm so startled I almost drop the tea cup I'm pretending to consider buying. I put it down and stick my head out the shop door. Sure enough, Mr. Jones is turning into the entrance of the Richmond Hotel.

"What time is it?" I ask one of the ladies shopping.

"Pardon me," she says, peering down the length of her nose.

"Time. What's the time?"

She blinks at my rudeness, but checks the pocket watch pinned to the waist of her unappealing brown dress. "Four o'clock."

Right on time. A sign of good character, or so I've been told.

I stroll into the tea room of the Richmond as if I've been there many times before. The place is almost full, ladies mostly having their tea. No one looks at me. No one but Mr. Jones, sitting at a table for two by the window, who gets to his feet with a smile. His cuffs are clean and he's wearing a different tie than he had on yesterday. The light coming in the windows shines off the big diamond in his stick pin.

I smile back, just a small smile, wouldn't do to look too pleased. I figure I look rather nice, too. I didn't want to wear the same dress I had on yesterday, so had to put on my other one. It has a large stain on the front, but I pinned a shawl in place to cover it. I'm too hot, but it can't be helped. What scraps of jewellery I have are so cheap Joshua never bothered to hawk them. My teardrop earrings with the small red stones put some colour into my face.

"I was afraid you wouldn't come," Mr. Jones says once we sit down. "You must have so many gentlemen wanting to make your acquaintance."

I scarcely know what to say to that. Sure there are six men for every woman in the Yukon, but most of the men are here for gold, not to find true love, and there are plenty of women in the cribs of Paradise Alley to provide whatever else they're looking for. From what I can see, it works the other way. The girls at the Savoy, the percentage girls and the dancers in the back row, are looking for a man to take care of them. Not necessarily to get married, but it's going to be a long cold winter.

I just smile, in the way Mrs. MacGillivray does when she's being secretive. It seems to be the right thing to do, as Mr. Jones blushes and smiles back.

The waiter, dressed in black with a long white apron, asks what we want. Mr. Jones orders tea and sandwiches for the both of us. Then he says, and I feel a shiver run up my arms, that we'll also have a plate of cakes.

We don't talk about much. Unlike most men trying to impress a lady, Mr. Jones is the quiet sort. Me, I'm afraid my accent's gonna slip so I keep my mouth shut. The tea's weak and the sandwiches are fish paste on gritty bread. The currants and raisins in the cake are few and far between, the milk's out of a can, but there's sugar for the tea and even fish paste's better than bacon and beans. I'm afraid Mr. Jones'll think me unladylike if I eat too much, but to be honest, I'm so hungry I don't much care. He orders a second plate of sandwiches once the cake's all gone.

We eat our food and sip our tea and don't say much.

At last it's time to go. Mr. Jones places money on the table for the bill, leaving, I can't help but notice, a large tip.

"That was such a substantial meal," he says when we're standing on the duckboard. "I need a stroll to settle it. Will you accompany me, Sarah?"

I've pretty much decided that if Mr. Jones wants payment for the food, I'll pay it. A girl's gotta survive, and the way my husband's going through my earnings and what supplies we have, I don't know if I'll last until I get the fare to the Outside.

"Sure," I says. "I mean, that would be most lovely."

He takes my arm and we stroll down to Front Street. We walk along the river like a proper courting couple. When we pass the Savoy, I sort of hope Mrs. MacGillivray or one of the front row performers sees us, and knows that I can be a lady of quality too. Then again, she's likely to think I'm a whore with a customer, so I steer Mr. Jones quickly past the dance hall.

"What time," he says, "do you need to be at work?"

"Midnight."

'Course if he wants to go back to my room that ain't on. Never mind Joshua, that place is such a dump Mr. Jones'll know the minute we come in sight of it that I'm no lady.

But he don't ask and we continue our stroll. We walk along the river front almost as far as where the Yukon meets up with the Klondike, and then turn inland towards the hills. It's a hot day with a bright yellow sun shining in a clear blue sky. I'm sweating under my shawl, but I don't dare take it off. It rained during the night and the streets are thick with mud. Sometimes the mud's so deep it comes up to a man's knees, or even a horse's. Sometimes the horses or donkeys get so stuck, they just stay there and die, and that's a pitiful sight. I was brought up on a farm, so I've seen birth and death, but some of the things we saw on our way to the Klondike scarcely bear thinking about.

'Course the mud smells to high heaven on a hot day like this one, but they've put boards down so people can walk along the street without having to step in too much of the muck. Makes it a right job trying to keep clothes clean, though.

We make a big circle of the town not talking about much. I try to walk slowly like a lady, rather than just a stupid girl with sore feet. After about two hours of this, Mr. Jones comes to a stop in front of a place named Jake's Restaurant. There's a big sign beside the door listing all sorts of wonderful things to eat—meat pies, steak, fruit, hot chocolate, apple and blueberry pies. I've heard the girls at work say there isn't none of that actually available. Beans and bacon, sardines and stewed tea's about the sum of it.

Mr. Jones says, "I'd enjoy a glass of lemonade. Would you like one, Sarah?"

Would I? I almost scream in delight. I remember my manners and say, "That would be most lovely, thank you."

Wonder of wonders, Jake does have lemonade. The glasses aren't none too clean, the lemonade comes out of a can and tastes mostly like water, but it smells nice and it's sorta cold.

There are only four tables in the whole place, and we take one by the window. When he finishes his drink, Mr. Jones pulls his watch out of his vest, opens it and checks the time. It's sure a nice watch. Real gold to my eyes. "It's getting close to eight," he says. "The time has gone so quickly."

OK, I think, here's the rub. Time to pay up, Sarah me girl.

"I'm sure you have to rest before your performance," he says, getting to his feet. He holds out his arm, assists me to rise, and we walk outside. "This has been very pleasant. Tea again tomorrow?"

"Sure," I says, forgetting to use my new accent in my astonishment.

He tips his hat, turns and walks away with a jaunty step. He's a small man, no taller than me at five foot seven, and slightly built. As I watch, he swings his cane in the air, nimbly dodges a half-starved dog being chased by two scruffy boys, and lifts his cap to a matronly lady with a bosom like the prow of a great ship. Then he turns the corner and is gone.

For the next two weeks this is my life. Mr. Jones stops at the Savoy at midnight and stays for an hour or two. He dances every dance with me, and seein' as to how I'm so popular, when he leaves, I've got men lining up for me, so that some nights I'm making almost twenty dollars. Imagine that! We have tea at the Richmond every afternoon, and then go for a walk, finishing up with lemonade at Jake's or some other place. Most days we walk uptown, towards the hills where the woods haven't yet been completely stripped away, because Mr. Jones says he likes to look at the wildflowers. The town's growing so fast, almost every day we have to walk further and further to get away from the tents and shacks people are making into homes.

We don't talk about personal stuff much. He's told me he's from New York and is in the Klondike for 'business'. I figure he owns a big mine and is here to make sure his managers don't try and get away with any fast stuff.

I don't tell him I'm married. I string some sort of line about being orphaned and an only child making my own way in the world. He says I am very brave.

And that's all Mr. Jones wants from me.

Joshua never asks where I get myself to in the afternoons, and I try to avoid him whenever I can. He looks like he's been fighting. And more than once, too. His handsome face is bashed up, he's lost a tooth, and he winces when he walks. I caught sight of him changing his shirt one afternoon: his side's so bruised up he looks like my brother Jimmy the time a horse kicked him full in the stomach. I didn't laugh much back on the farm, but I sure laughed that day, I can tell you.

For the first time since we've been married, Joshua stops trying to get at me under the covers and I'm so pleased at that I don't wonder why.

By the end of the two weeks, I'm thinking it's time for Joshua to leave town. Tea and lemonade's all well and good, but my feet are hurting something awful from all that darned walking and then dancing all night on top of it. I expect Mr. Jones to make a proposal and Joshua is an obstacle I don't need.

Then at the end of the second week, just as I'm beginning to fear me and Mr. Jones will be walking forever, he says he has some news to tell me. We're up past the last row of houses, and can hear the sound of hammers and saws hard at it pushing the town further up the sides of the hill. That's another thing I hate about Dawson: sawdust everywhere. If it rains, it settles the dust, but that makes mud. If it don't rain, the streets dry up, but the sawdust gets so thick sometimes you have to brush off your clothes almost every day.

Mr. Jones pulls out a white handkerchief—real white, you don't see that in Dawson much—and dusts off a large boulder like a gentleman. He gestures for me to sit down. I sit primly, my hands folded in my lap, a small smile on my face. It won't look good to be too happy before he's even popped the question. Oh, I'm not a fool. I don't expect Mr. Jones is about to propose anything legal. I figure an arrangement'll be good enough—I'll move in with him, keep house for him, keep him warm over the winter. He'll provide for me and leave me with a nice present when it's spring and time to part.

Probably better than an offer of marriage. That way I won't have to tell him I'm already married.

I smile up at Mr. Jones.

"I like helping out hard-working young people," he says. "And as a bonus, I've enjoyed your company very much, Sarah. I'd like to give you a little gift before I go."

I hear the words *gift* and *go*.

He digs into his coat pocket. He pulls out a piece of paper, and holds it in one hand while rummaging around looking for something. "Ticket for the evening boat. Ah, here it is." He puts the ticket and paper back in his pocket and hands me a small box, wrapped with a nice red ribbon. I untie the ribbon and open the box with shaking fingers. It's a single cube of sugar. I stare at it, not even bothered that my mouth's hanging open.

"Because you've been so sweet," he says, "giving up your time to keep company with a lonely old man. Now I must be off. I have to get back to my rooms and pick up my luggage."

"You're leaving," I says at last.

"I don't want to be trapped here when winter sets in. I've been away from Mary and the children and grandchildren long enough as it is."

Still smiling, he holds out his hand to help me to my feet. "I'm looking forward to telling Mary about the charming lady who made my time in Dawson a pleasant one."

I look down at the open box. One cube of sugar. That's all I'm going to get. I can hear blood pounding in my ears.

I ignore his hand and start to stand up, ready to give Mr. Jones a cuff to the ear and a right piece of my mind. I step on a rock and feel a sharp jab as it punches through the thin sole of my boot. Gasping with shock and pain, I drop back to the boulder. My hand touches a rock. Without even thinking, my fingers close over that rock, I drop the sugar box, grab Mr. Jones's outstretched arm, and use it to pull me to my feet. I've got a lot of momentum behind me as well as pure rage. I swing the rock high overhead and bring it down on the side of his head.

He goes down with a grunt and lies still.

I stand over him, breathing heavily. A large patch of blood begins to soak into the dirt under his head.

I look around. We're tucked into a copse of stubby trees which have miraculously escaped the town's appetite for wood. No one else is in sight. I drop to my knees and feel Mr. Jones's neck. I was raised on a farm, remember. I know the difference between a dead body and a live one.

I dig quickly through his pockets. One steamship ticket, destination Seattle, and a letter. I stuff letter and ticket in my pocket and continue the search. He isn't wearing the diamond stick pin today, but his pocket watch and chain are gold. A billfold with more dollars than I've ever seen in my life, and a hefty pouch. I open the pouch, my heart beating fast 'cause I can guess what it contains. A handful of gold nuggets and a good bit of dust. My mind's moving as fast as ever it has. If I can get Mr. Jones's body down to the river or into the wilderness, and dump it, it might never be found. But I can hardly carry a dead body up into the hills or through town to the river.

I could walk away, leave him for someone to find, but plenty of folks have seen us on our daily rendezvous. They'd point to me right away.

I could say it was an accident. The Mounties wouldn't hang a woman just 'cause she'd been there when her companion fell and hit his head.

But I'd have to hand over the gold and the money. I look at the steamship ticket: it's made out to Mr. Albert Jones. Easy enough to change the Mr. to Mrs. and take his place. As soon as someone comes across the body and I'm reported missing, the police'll be looking for me. But there ain't no telegraph or telephone, and I'll be travelling faster on the boat than anyone on foot.

I've got a ticket to the Outside and enough money to get home to Manitoba, even to travel in some style. No time to go back to my room and get my things, but that's no matter. Except for the pitifully small bit of money hidden in the wall, I own nothing I want to keep. I can buy anything I need in Seattle.

With a great deal of effort I manage to roll most of Mr. Jones behind the boulder, enough anyway that he won't be seen by a casual passer-by. Some blood's splashed on the bottom of my dress, but I rub dust into it so I don't look no worse than anyone else.

I walk through town with my head high and my step firm. I know where there's a shop what sells suitcases and valises. I've got nothing to put in a suitcase, but figure they'll take notice of me on the ship if I don't have any luggage.

Mr. Jones's gold dust is good. I leave the shop with a new reticule, a large valise with leather trim, and a hat box decorated with a beautiful flower design.

I get to the boat as it's boarding. Anywhere else in the world, I'd be asked why I'm travelling alone without much luggage. But in Dawson, no one pays attention to anyone else, and I board after a cursory glance at my ticket from the steward.

I settle myself into my room, the like of which I've never been in before, kick off the hated boots and bounce on the bed a couple o' times to check the mattress. As I rub my feet, I vow that the first thing I'm gonna do when I get to Seattle is to buy a good pair of shoes. Bugger the cost. I fall back onto the bed in a fit of giggles.

I wash and fix my hair as best I can and take myself onto the deck to have a look around. I'm standing at the railing, watching the wilderness drift by. It's right chilly and the snowline's far down the mountainside. Winter's coming and I'm getting out just in time.

Two gentlemen doff their hats to me and I say, "Good evening," in my new accent. Won't my parents and my brothers think I'm grand when I arrive at the farm speaking like a lady and wearing the latest in fashion?

"Biggest strike this year, they're saying," the first gentleman says to the second.

"I figured all the good places were taken."

"So did everyone else, but that's probably the last one. He just got lucky, that young man, although I heard he raised the last bit of the money by bare-knuckle boxing. He was able to buy the claim for pennies because everyone said the Black Creek didn't have a speck of gold in it. But Jones told him where to look, and he believed in Jones."

"Good man, Jones. They say he's got a better nose for the metal than any man alive, and enough decency not to cheat anyone by telling them their claim's useless to take it off their hands."

My ears twitch at the mention of Jones, but the men move away and I can't hear no more. I flutter my fingers at them in the way I've seen Mrs. MacGillivray do at the Savoy.

I go back to my room to practise my new accent in front of the mirror. It would be easier if I had something to read aloud from rather than just talking to myself. I remember the letter tucked in with Mr. Jones's steamship ticket and pull it out of my reticule.

I unfold the paper. I recognize the childish handwriting right away.

> *"Al,*
>
> *Thanks again for looking after Sarah. With her happy and busy, I've been able to concentrate on our business without listening to her harping on as if a husband ain't got the right to use his wife's earnings to improve their lot. Your advice was spot on and I just got word they've found gold, right where you said to look. I'm gonna name the claim Miss Sarah. Sounds better than The Black Creek, don't you think?*
>
> *Your grateful friend,*
> *Joshua Richards."*

About Vicki Delany

    "It's a crime not to read Delany," so says the *London Free Press*.

    Vicki Delany is one of Canada's most varied and prolific crime writers. Her popular *Constable Molly Smith series* (including *In the Shadow of the Glacier* and *A Cold White Sun*) from Poisoned Pen Press have received starred reviews from *Publishers Weekly* and *Library Journal*. She is the author of a light-hearted historical series, (*Gold Digger, Gold Web*). as well as suspense novels including *Burden of Memory* and *More than Sorrow. A Winter Kill*, was shortlisted for the 2012 Arthur Ellis Award for best novella.

    Vicki is a member of the Capital Crime Writers, The Writers Union of Canada, and is on the board of the Crime Writers of Canada and the Wolfe Island Scene of the Crime Festival. She has been chosen as Canadian guest of honour for Bloody Words 2014.

Connect with Vicki at:
http://www.vickidelany.com/
http://klondikeandtrafalgar.blogspot.ca/
FaceBook: Vicki Delany
Twitter: @vickidelany
www.mesdamesofmayhem.com

Sugar 'N' Spice

by Joan O'Callaghan

My neighbour's golden retriever, Molson, found Becky Robinson's naked body under a dock while chasing a piece of driftwood. The fifteen-year-old had been beaten, my neighbour confided later that evening.

The finger of suspicion pointed at Henri Charbonneau.

Henri was a French teacher at Lakeview High School in Hidden Harbour where I taught English. A relatively new arrival from Montreal, he was strikingly handsome in that particularly Gallic way. He always looked as if he needed a shave. His straight brown hair was just a tad long and fell over his right eye. Tall and lean, he wore his clothes as if he were in the pages of *Gentleman's Quarterly* instead of a musty classroom. The girls, and even the women teachers, described him as drop-dead gorgeous. Unfailingly courteous, Henri was utterly professional with his coterie of admirers. The morning Becky's body was found, he called the school office to say he had a family emergency to deal with and would be away for several days.

Chaos reigned at school the next day. The police took over the office of our principal, Ellie Tomlinson. Grief counsellors set up shop in the Student Services Department and students poured in to weep, be comforted, and miss classes. Becky's friends Crystal, Jenn and Madison spent the entire day there, except for intervals when they were seen in the halls and cafeteria, loudly sniffing, eyes red.

Schools are small communities and Lakeview was soon awash in ugly rumours, stoked by Becky's friends and Henri's absence, rumours that placed Becky with Henri. The rest was easy to guess. Before long the entire town was whispering that Henri had raped Becky, and then killed her to hush up his crime. It was all nonsense, of course. Henri would never lay a finger on Becky.

Becky and her friends were all students in my Grade 10 English class. I didn't much care for Becky. And I didn't like her three friends either. They were pretty in a cookie-cutter way, with long blonde hair, makeup, too-tight jeans and clingy tops that left little to the imagination. It didn't help that they were arrogant, lazy and generally obnoxious. Still, I was shocked beyond words, and grieved for a young life cut off so early and so violently.

Of course, the police spoke to me. I was Becky's English teacher and knew Henri better than most. The English Department shared an office with Modern Languages. Henri's desk was next to mine and our timetables were the same.

Did Henri ever mention Becky? Had he shown any interest in her? I shook my head. Henri, I told them, never mentioned Becky.

Was he married? Did he have a girlfriend? Henri never discussed his private life.

Did I have any idea where he might have gone? I shrugged.

Classes were cancelled so everyone could attend the memorial service. The funeral would come later, after the police released the body. The church was filled to overflowing. The entire staff and student body must have been there. In the second pew, right behind Becky's parents, Crystal, Madison, and Jenn sobbed loudly throughout the service.

The minister ended by quoting from William Blake's *The Sick Rose*. In what seemed to me a thinly veiled reference to Henri, his deep voice rang out: *"...his dark secret love does thy life destroy."* I bit my lip.

Things at school returned to normal. That is, routines were re-established. After such a tragedy, how could things be normal?

I noticed Becky's friends huddling in corners whispering. They were distracted and inattentive. Soon after the memorial service, they crowded around my desk after I dismissed the class, and asked if there'd been any word from Monsieur Charbonneau.

I shook my head. "Why?"

They looked at each other and shrugged.

"Just curious," Jenn said. "The police should have caught him by now. Perv." She sniffed and turned to her friends, who nodded in agreement.

"You're sure of that? In this country, a person's innocent until proven guilty. There could be any number of reasons for Monsieur Charbonneau's absence." I began stuffing books and papers into my briefcase.

"Oh, we're sure." The corner of Crystal's mouth quirked upward.

"How so?" I couldn't help myself. What could these three possibly know?

They looked at each other again and as if on cue, stepped closer, almost circling the desk where I sat. Then Madison spoke. "We all know he had the hots for her. He was always staring at her and looking down her top."

They giggled. Jenn picked up the narrative. "Yeah. He used to brush against her boobs—oops!" She clapped her hand over her mouth. "Sorry. I mean her chest. Like this." She leaned over me and thrust her chest out so her breasts almost brushed against my head. I pushed my chair back, stood and stared at her. The girls snickered.

I dropped my eyes to hide my discomfort. "Becky must have imagined that."

"Oh no," they said together in chorus. "The night she died, he asked her to meet him."

I took a step back and appraised them coolly. "How do you know all this?"

"She told us. He said he wanted to talk to her about her test mark. She was failing French, so she figured she better go. But she was really antsy about meeting him."

"What time did she meet him?" I held my breath.

"About eight. It was just starting to get dark. Probably on purpose so people wouldn't see them or recognize them." This from Madison. The others nodded vigorously.

"Did you tell the police?"

"Of course. That's why they're looking for him." Crystal blinked, no doubt trying to look honest and sincere.

Time to end this. "Thanks, girls."

They trooped out of the classroom. I waited a few minutes then gathered up my case, locked the door, and headed down to my car in the parking lot. Vern Stemler, the head of the Phys.Ed. Department, caught up with me.

"Thought I'd have to blast this to get your attention." He chuckled and fingered the whistle hanging from a cord around his neck. "Saw you talking to the terrible three when I walked past your classroom. Good thing you had the door open."

I slowed my step. "I always keep the door open when I'm speaking to students."

"Can't be too cautious. That bunch is toxic."

"Tell me about it. They could give the witches in *Macbeth* a run for their money."

Vern said, "Remember Dan Clark?"

I thought for a moment. "The young teacher who was helping coach football? Left at Christmas?"

"That's him." Vern stopped and turned to me. "He left because of them."

"Really? What happened?" I was beginning to get a sick feeling about this.

"Last fall, one day after practice, he was putting away the equipment. Crystal suddenly appeared. She walked over to him bold as brass and rubbed up against him. He jumped away from her but she started grabbing him, if you get my meaning. He told her to stop, that he'd report her. She just smirked and asked who'd believe him. It was like a signal. Out jumped Jenn and Madison. They said they'd seen the whole thing and would have him charged with sexual assault, if he didn't give them a hundred dollars each. Madison showed him her cell phone. She'd taken a picture of Crystal up close against him. Dan said anyone seeing it would think he was feeling her up."

I stopped and stared at Vern. "I thought he left because he wanted to be closer to his family."

"That's the story he gave Ellie."

Vern continued. "I bumped into him at a coaches' conference a couple of months back. He told me the whole story over a few beers. He was terrified they'd ruin his career or keep coming back for more money."

"You said Crystal, Madison and Jenn. Where was Becky? Wasn't she part of that group?"

"Not when that happened. I saw her leaving practice with Greg Hayes. They were an item."

"Was she still going with him when she died?"

"Yeah. We were away at a tournament. He just about went off the deep end when he heard. At least, Clark's got a job in Hamilton. Wanna know what I think? You look around, you'll find more guys had the same experience. Take it easy." And he loped off in the direction of his SUV.

I drove home slowly, thinking about what Vern said. I poured a glass of red wine, put Beethoven on the CD-player and settled into my favourite armchair to think. I knew Henri hadn't killed Becky.

The next morning I stood by the classroom door after I'd dismissed my senior class. I stopped Greg Hayes as he was leaving. "Do you have a moment?" He nodded and followed me to my desk.

"I'm very sorry about Becky. I understand you were," I groped for the right word, "close."

He dropped his head, but I saw the tear that coursed down his face. Angrily, he swiped at it.

"It's OK to cry. You've suffered a terrible loss." I paused. "I have to ask you something."

I continued, "The night Becky died—do you know where she was?"

He jerked his head up.

"I know you were at a tournament. I just wondered if you knew where she was. She wasn't with Mr. Charbonneau, was she." It was a statement, not a question.

Greg's face turned white and he wouldn't meet my eyes.

"You have to tell the truth. I know you're innocent. But so is Mr. Charbonneau. Where was Becky the night she died? Who was she with?"

"I—I—" he faltered. His hand covered his eyes and he dropped into a chair.

I waited.

And then, sobbing and choking, he poured out his story. He thought Becky was on the pill. The trip to Toronto for the abortion took most of the money he'd put away for university. Becky wasn't supposed to tell anyone.

"But she did tell someone," I said.

He nodded. "Crystal, Jenn, and Madison. They came to me and to Becky separately and threatened to tell our parents if we didn't give them money."

"I thought they were Becky's friends."

"She thought so, too. I guess that's why she told them."

"So what did you do?"

"We said no. Becky told them if they said anything to our parents, she'd go to the police and tell them about the blackmail. She said she'd give details of what they did to Mr. Clark." Greg said he thought they'd pulled the same stunt on a couple of other male teachers, but he couldn't be sure.

He left, and a few minutes later after organizing some materials for my afternoon class, I followed. I was locking the classroom door when Madison sidled up to me, her eyes wide, her facial features arranged to communicate concern.

"I saw you talking to Greg. Is he OK?"

"What do you think?"

"He's had such a bad shock. We're really worried about him. He seemed pretty upset when he was talking to you."

"How do you know? Were you spying on him?" After hearing Greg's story, I was in no mood to play games with the girls.

Her face turned red. "I would never do that. I was walking past the classroom and saw him sitting there talking to you. I just wondered how he's doing, like if he said anything."

"He said a lot of things. Why are you so curious?"

"Forget it." She spat out the words and stalked away.

I watched her go. I'll bet you're worried, I thought. In fact, I think you're scared.

I could feel the corners of my mouth turn up in a small smile of satisfaction. But it's when people feel threatened that they're dangerous, and I was under no illusions about my own safety. I went to Ellie's office, closed the door and told her what Greg had told me, and my suspicions. She placed a call to our police chief. When I got home, I made a phone call of my own.

Later that evening, I was marking essays at home when there was a knock at my door. It was Madison.

"Can I come in? I need to talk to you."

I blocked the doorway. "We can talk here. What's on your mind?"

"What did Greg Hayes tell you?"

"Is that what this is about?"

"He's a liar and a sleaze."

"You don't even know what we were talking about, so how do you know he's a liar? Maybe we were discussing his English mark."

There was a movement in the bushes.

"Come on out Jenn, Crystal. I know you're there."

Two hands pushed the shrubs aside and Jenn emerged. She turned to pick up something from the ground. Metal gleamed in the porch light. She'd brought a golf club.

"If he said anything about us, it's all lies." She gripped the club. "And you better not say anything either. We don't care if you are a teacher."

I took a step back and stumbled against the doorframe. I put my hand on it to steady myself.

Jenn swung the club menacingly.

"A bit dark to be playing golf, isn't it?" Without waiting for an answer, I turned to the bushes on the other side of the porch. "And what have you brought to the party, Crystal? The same weapons you used on poor Becky?"

There was a crash as Crystal leapt from her hiding place and swung a baseball bat, missing me but hitting the large flower pot by the door and smashing it. I jumped to one side and ducked instinctively to avoid being hit by flying dirt and shards of terracotta.

The noise alerted Molson who began barking furiously and growling.

"You don't want to mess with that dog. He's the one that found Becky's body. He knows your scent." It was a long shot but it worked. They looked at each other. That moment was all the time I needed. I shouted, "Call the police."

Lights went on next door as my neighbour stepped into the yard to quiet Molson. The girls didn't wait. They ran, leaving the club and bat behind. From behind me, Henri touched my arm. "The police are on their way. I heard everything."

Once we'd given our statements to the police, Henri and I shared a bottle of wine and toasted our future. His trip to Calgary had been a success. They are hiring teachers there. Henri already has a job for next September and I have an interview lined up. We'll be able to live together and teach in two different schools.

Small towns like Hidden Harbour are not ready for a gay couple to live openly.

About Joan O'Callaghan

Joan O'Callaghan is a recipient of the Golden Apple Award from Queen's University Faculty of Education for Excellence in Teaching, was named Professor of the Year by OISE/UT Students Council, as well as Most Engaging English Instructor and Most Inspirational Instructor.

She is the author of three educational books as well as two e-shorts: *George* and *For Elise* (Carrick Publishing).

Her short story *Stooping to Conquer* appeared in the 2012 Anthology *EFD1: Starship Goodwords* (Carrick Publishing).

Connect with Joan at:
FaceBook: Joan O'Callaghan
Twitter: @JoanOcallaghan
www.mesdamesofmayhem.com

The Three R's

by Catherine Astolfo

Chief Dan Mahdahbee felt very proud of his accomplishment right up until the moment the skeletons appeared. As a spiritual man, not a superstitious one, his reaction was not one of fear or suspicion. He was simply pissed off.

Dan was not a typical chief in many ways. Always adorned in heavy gold jewelry and designer clothing, whether traditional native or more modern attire, he was unashamed to show off his personal wealth. He had a great head for business, made lots of money, employed many people, and felt he was entitled to flaunt it if he so desired.

On a momentous occasion such as this one, he was spectacularly dressed in a flamboyant turquoise blue shirt, white leggings and a headdress made of eagle down. Over his shirt, he wore a knitted vest that had been in his family for many generations. Its bright white and sea-blue beads formed patterns that resembled small birds. Beautiful embroidery and frills decorated his legs and arms. Around his large waist he wore a sash with the emblem of a bear etched clearly in brown and white. To complete the outfit, a wing-like garment made of white and blue dyed feathers was draped over his shoulders.

Anyone who lived in the twin communities of Burchill and the Sahsejewon Reserve was used to Dan's excesses, such as his legendary Gucci watch, and accepted them as part of the enigma that was their beloved chief. Right now, however, Dan's villagers were the guests. It had taken a little while for the community of Vryheid to get used to him, but embrace him they had. His generous, intelligent personality paired with his ability to follow through on a vision had won everyone's approval during the weeks they'd been visiting the region.

When the human remains interrupted the party, Chief Dan was one of the dignitaries leading the parade of dancers, accompanied by drummers and horns, around a huge circle. They had stopped, as planned, in front of the old church where the flag of friendship was to be raised. The pennant had been designed by Burchill's most famous painter, William Langford Taylor, and sewn by artisans from the chief's store. The symbols, which celebrated both black and native history, were created as leaves on a tree, in colours that no tree had ever really sported even in the depths of a Canadian autumn. It was a striking, breathtaking emblem, resplendent when seen up close and eye-catching from afar. Unfortunately, the flag was not destined to fly that day.

***

"We dreamt of space. The wind free to whip our hair into veils or tickle our noses. In winter, its bitter nips and punches. The trees, our ancestors, speaking to us with their soft woody voices. Animals showing us the way."

Her eyes were hooded by folds of life but their granite brown shone like sunlit streaks through rock. The old woman's eyes were what attracted the child in the first place. They had so many layers of thought and experience. Next to that mesmerizing gaze, her voice was nearly as captivating with its flat, round tones and slow paced phrases.

When she told her stories, time ceased to have meaning. They were both transported to a past that was now more alive than present or future, for elder and youngster alike.

"Here there were walls. They loomed over us like mountains with no peaks. Dull green hallway tunnels. Everything echoed so even a whisper could be heard far ahead. Like the mountains and lakes where a whisper carries to ears far away. But the meaning was so different. Being heard meant punishment, not connection to life. Instead pain was the result."

***

The track around which the parade cavorted had been carved out of earth that had once been a village. Almost sixty years ago Vryheid had burned to the ground, leaving only the charred remains of wooden shacks that, until the fire, had lasted for a century. Slowly nature took back the space, covering it with flourishing trees, bushes and weeds. The only sign of human interference, after a few years, had been an ancient chapel and a few tilted cemetery stones. The church stood on a slight hill, apart from the rows of homes, which was perhaps the reason the conflagration hadn't reached it.

A few years ago, spearheaded by the nearby Burford Museum and Archives, Vryheid had been restored. Now the celebration track, the touched-up chapel and a reconstructed shack were open for tourism and powwows. Under the auspices of the town of Burford, revels—like the one in which Dan and his troupe were participating today—were common. This gathering, however, was quite different in its scope.

The event had been billed as an enormous coup for native, white and black leaders in Southern Ontario. Their multi-year planning had finally come to fruition. The indigenous people, the slaves who had found freedom in their midst, and those in the white community who'd never let colour get in the way, were congregated to celebrate and affirm.

The skeletons added an element the leaders had not counted on.

The group of dancing, stomping, skipping and jumping celebrators had gathered in a tight knot in front of the church, just at the edge of the small hill. A tall flagpole had been cemented into the ground, to purposely lift the banner above the treetops, so that on a clear day, it would be seen miles away. Three other flags fluttered in the wind, testimony to a previous celebration like this one.

The audience, who were scattered around on risers built for the occasion, or seated on lawn chairs, or the backs of trucks and campers, clapped and waited enthusiastically for the flag raising. Some had joined the dancers. They bowed and dipped with the rhythm of the hand drums, or whirled to the sound of sax and trumpet.

It was a gorgeous, sunny day with no hint of humidity. White clouds etched a clear blue sky. The music, the soft clean breeze, the sounds of the river in the distance, and the incredible colours of the ceremonial costumes, all combined to make the people boisterous and happy. Most of them stood, swayed, jumped or pushed toward the parade in groups.

The Grand River ran wildly through this area, winding deep and shallow along the shores. The combination of soft rock and a tumultuous river resulted in damp ground throughout the former village. Everyone was soon splattered with reddish muck, but no one appeared to care.

The people on the risers felt the first movements in the ground but they dismissed them as reverberations from the celebration. The rumbling moved like an enormous underground snake, wiggling past the groups at lightning speed. Most participants were oblivious until the wave hit the chapel. Built a century ago, the structure was naturally a little unsteady. Restorations had been somewhat superficial.

Although the earthquake was more of an aftershock from the epicenter south of Hamilton, a few miles away, it was enough to shake the church's steeple loose from its moorings. Suddenly, old brick and stone crumbled, striking the flat rock steps around it and breaking into small bits. Debris, luckily harmless, tumbled downhill to land at the feet of the dancers.

However, mixed in with the dirt and ancient building blocks were fragments and larger pieces of bone. No one grasped the situation until a skull, amazingly intact despite its fall, rolled down the embankment and halted at Chief Dan Mahdahbee's feet.

Edgar Brennan, the Chief Superintendent of Burchill's Ontario Provincial Police Department, reacted immediately. He moved people back by the sheer force of his voice, waving them away from the scene before anyone could trample the discovery by mistake. Two Brant County police constables, who had been assigned to provide security, came rushing forward to assist him. Although there was some chaos—and a great deal of talking and muttering—people were generally cooperative.

The performers hung around, unsure whether or not the show must go on, while most of the spectators began to flow back to their vehicles. As a consequence, the little site of Vryheid was shortly filled with silent, colourful dancers, lined up facing the activity at the church, like birds asleep on a high wire. At this moment they should have been in flight, whirling and flashing in the sunlight. The drums should have been rhythmic and inspiring instead of deathly quiet: some lay abandoned on the ground. It should have been a celebration of the unique intermingling of native, black and white histories, the way Chief Dan and his colleagues had imagined, dreamed and planned for over three years. Instead they were all fixated on a jumble of bones, dirt and stone.

***

"Most of all I missed my mother."

The child's heart constricted. She, too, had suffered trauma. A withdrawal of maternal love in a very different way, but no less painful.

"My mother was an affectionate woman, more demonstrative than most. She liked to touch, to hug and kiss. Sometimes she embarrassed my father with her outgoing love. But never me or my brother and sister. We purred like kittens. We read books with arms around her or leaning into her. She made up stories, too. Tales of her childhood and her mother and father, whom we had never met. They came to life for us through her words. Soon those hallways removed the sound of her voice and the shape of her face. It is my biggest regret. I have no pictures, no movies the way you young people have today. I have only my poor memory."

The girl shivered in the hot sunlight. How she wished there were no pictures of her birth mother. No television shows, no newspapers, no permanent record of the havoc that woman's malevolence had wrought.

Here was a different evil. One that separated loving parents from their children with no thought of how that would damage little hearts.

***

Someone searched a local news outlet on a smart phone and confirmed the earthquake.

"The epicenter was far south of Hamilton," the dancer told them all. "Vryheid was in a direct line, so the tremors were pretty strong here in comparison with some other towns."

Although an earthquake had occurred two years ago in the area, Ontarians were not accustomed to the phenomenon. Tremors were normally mild and caused no damage. The relayed news report drove the remainder of spectators to scurry home. Fearful of further rumblings, they fled back to town for access to television or to gather loved ones who hadn't accompanied them to the festival.

Emily Taylor was frantic. During the parade, she had been sitting on the VIP dais with her husband, William Langford Taylor. As the designer of the flag, Will was to assist with its raising. He was to join the festivities by presenting the emblem to the various chiefs and mayors who had gathered. No one else had reached the platform before the quake.

The dais, constructed of wooden planks and two-by-fours, sat directly on the ground in front of the hillock. As a result, it rumbled quite loudly when the earth shook underneath it. Both Emily and Will leapt to their feet before the church spilled its contents. They simultaneously swung their heads toward the stands—and their two daughters.

Carly, her reddish hair glinting in the sunlight under a straw bonnet, was easily spotted where she sat in a lawn chair at the foot of the first bench. Years ago she had lost both her feet in a fire. Even though she was pretty sturdy on her artificial limbs, she was not comfortable climbing up the wooden steps. A few of her friends had stayed with her, but as they moved off with their parents, Carly began to make her way toward Emily and William—alone.

Cate was nowhere to be seen. The tall, willowy blonde girl had been sitting close to her sister, but she was no longer visible.

Normally Emily might not have been so worried. If they had been home in Burchill, the gathering would have been full of friends and neighbours. Cate might have gone home with one of the groups of friends who'd come to Vryheid, but surely they would have checked in with Emily or Will first.

Over the summer, the teenager had pulled several vanishing acts and though William disagreed with her about this, Emily was sure Cate had been lying about her whereabouts.

By the time Carly reached her parents, the majority of families had swarmed toward the parking venue further up the road. The site was deserted. Only the gaily-dressed performers, two chiefs and three police officers remained.

"Where's Cate?" Emily asked, more harshly than she intended, as Will gathered Carly in a bear hug.

"She was right..." The freckle-faced girl turned toward the stands, which were now empty, and looked back at her parents with a frown.

Carly had grown quite tall in the last couple of years. She was slim, with startling blue-green eyes and reddish blonde hair. Her body had begun its metamorphosis into adolescence. No longer board straight, she had formed hips and breasts and was becoming more conscious of her body. She was a talkative, assertive child whose confrontational style had led her into many a conflict, but had also allowed her to overcome what might have been a devastating handicap.

Carly had adjusted fairly well to the lightweight, durable feet that had been constructed for her long legs and high energy level. A determined, stubborn nature caused her to work hard at everything she did, including gaining control over her disability. She wasn't as classically beautiful as her older sister, but Carly was extremely attractive, with her wide mouth and ready laugh. Right now her straw hat was at an angle. Her bright pink top and blue jean shorts were tinged with sweat.

"I don't know where she went," Carly said. "She wasn't far up on the stands. Maybe she went with one of the other girls."

"Maybe," Emily mumbled. "But she should've told us. Will, I'm going back to the house. Do you want to stay here?"

"I'll check with Edgar first. See if he needs any help."

William was a tall handsome man whose deep brown eyes were enhanced by a thick head of dark hair shot with grey and a face that showed few wrinkles. He was quiet and introspective, a great listener and a talented artist. Today his green shirt was printed with white feathers and stripes, a work of art he had created himself.

"Was that really an earthquake, Mem?" Carly was asking.

"Apparently so," Emily answered. "That's why I wish I knew where Cate is. I want to get back and see what's happened."

"Let's get a closer look at those bones," Carly suggested. "I wanna see what came out of that church. If I had a cell phone, I could've taken a picture."

"You know how your Dad feels about that."

Speaking about the cell phone, not her daughter's wish to photograph bones.

If we had a cell phone, I could call Cate right now, Emily thought, but she would never say such a thing aloud to her willful daughter.

"Anyway, honey, I don't think the police want us near the scene."

Emily stood with one hand on her daughter's shoulder, as though she could quell her morbid curiosity. They watched as the police officers scurried around the site performing their own kind of rituals. Edgar spoke briefly to William who, thank goodness, began to make his way back to his family.

Her eyes on her husband, Emily wasn't paying enough attention to Carly. The girl suddenly darted straight for the crime scene tape. William caught up with their daughter just as she turned and pointed.

"That skeleton is awfully small," she announced in a loud, authoritative voice. "It must be the remains of a child."

The Taylors had been staying in a beautiful home just outside the village. The house, owned by a family who was away for the summer, was extremely comfortable and homey despite its pretentious appearance. There was no sign of Cate in any of the rooms, no indication that she had even dropped by after the quake. Emily had a difficult time stemming her sense of foreboding and panic.

Carly began to telephone Cate's friends. Amidst the talk about the earthquake and the skeletons, a little information emerged. One friend, Yasmine, noticed that Cate ran off toward the forest after the bones appeared.

"OK, now I'm worried too," William finally admitted. "What the hell could she have been thinking?"

Irritated and anxious, Emily was abnormally sharp with her husband. "I told you there has been something going on with her. She's been behaving strangely since we got here. We're missing something."

Adopted by the Taylors a few years ago, Catherine and Carly Sanderson had suffered horrific trauma that, despite the ongoing counseling, kept Emily and William vigilant. Probably even more than normal for parents of teenagers, they watched for any signs of harmful behaviour.

Emily was the worst for this and they both knew it, so sometimes Will had to play devil's advocate.

"You're probably right, but that's not going to help just now," he said quietly, with the calmness that often left Emily exasperated.

However, she had to concede that he was right this time. She took a deep breath. "OK. Carly, have you got any ideas?"

"She didn't tell me anything was going on. I've been so busy I didn't even notice."

"Maybe we should start searching the woods," Emily said. "Could Yasmine pinpoint the direction?"

"I can ask her."

"Let's do it," William said. "We can at least try searching ourselves before we call the police."

Carly's face paled as they all felt the first reverberations of genuine fear. Armed with a few vague facts from Yasmine, William and Emily set off toward the woods and the river. Carly stayed home in case her sister appeared. Once again, she reminded them that smart phones would have come in handy.

***

"Some of the nuns were nice to us. I learned to earn a gentle touch by following the rules, by studying hard. I was a smart girl, something like you, I suspect."

By now the girl and the woman had formed a close bond through words and pictures. The child sketched while the elder spoke. Page after page showed the wrinkled countenance, the cloud of white hair and soft brown skin wrapped in blankets in the middle of the day.

"The three R's, they told us, were the most important things in life. I became obsessed with learning. It was my source, my motivation. I excelled. Got a job with the white man. Joined hands with the devil.

Only later in my days did I recognize that the three R's were really re-education, rules and religion."

"What about your brother and sister?"

The girl was becoming used to questioning. She would sift through the elder's guarded way of speaking to mine the details.

"They never made friends with English words. They couldn't do it. My sister wet the bed every night even though she quickly knew the pain of beatings that would follow."

"Maybe she couldn't help it."

A slow nod was all she would sometimes receive, but this time the old woman gave more.

"I think the pain became her obsession. It was her way of keeping a distance from the devil. A reminder that she would never be one of them. My brother, too. He did it in his own way. He withdrew. Made no waves, caused no trouble, spoke to no one."

***

Perversely the perfect weather held despite the fact that the ground had been given a good shake. Emily and William trotted along the road toward the area where Yasmine had seen Cate disappear. Carved out of a tunnel of ancient trees that intertwined above, blocking sun and scenery, the Old Vryheid Trail was more path and less road these days. Another entrance to the village had been constructed a few years ago.

Over the last two months the family of four had often strolled together under the ancient branches, feeling the cooling shade and breeze. Birds sang, gossiped and flitted back and forth overhead. Squirrels chattered loudly, while every once in a while another wildlife character would inadvertently show itself: deer, fox, a rabbit family.

Emily couldn't help but think the worst. If she lost Cate, how would she recover? How could any parent stand the disappearance of a child? The ache was already there though nothing had happened. She shivered under the tunnel of trees and grasped Will's hand. Trying hard to shake off the worry, she concentrated on the trees.

"Yasmine said she raced toward the tunnel. A couple of times before, she's seen Cate walk down a pathway from here. How on earth are we going to find it?"

William squeezed Emily's hand. "I don't know. I just think we'll know it when we see it."

He was right. A few moments later they spied an opening that led away from the road through the trees. They had to walk single file, following greenery that had been trampled but not obliterated. The tree line ended in a grassy meadow that sloped down and became a cliff over the river. They could hear fierce rapids close by.

To their left, a huge clump of bushes and stumpy trees formed a barrier that resembled a circular buttress. Emily and William looked at each other. Something drew them toward the fortress of green.

***

The woman's eyes became less focused as the summer progressed. In the deep heat of August she was cool and clammy. Her arms wrinkled up like an orange peel left too long in the sun. When the girl came to visit, the elder no longer shared in the proffered feast of cookies or apple slices. Even the bottle of ginger ale, up to now her favorite, was refused.

She began to wander in her stories. They no longer made much sense.

"The horned panther prowled the halls."

"What was happening, Akhso?" The old woman had suggested the name, almost as a gift, and the girl used it without knowing its meaning. In turn, she had been called Keshini.

The elder's eyes fluttered, then turned on the youngster with a light she'd not seen before.

"Death arrived. It stalked the tunnels. Took away the breath. Eyes empty. Spirits gone."

Once she pointed toward the old village. "You see. They are near."

The girl boarded the bus and rode out to the museum in Brantford. Compared to the small towns she frequented, this was a city. A bit disconcerting at first. The stop, however, was right outside the dark stone gates. She walked along the shaded driveway toward an enormous red brick building. Using the old woman's eyes, she saw the faceless windows, the peaked dormers, the cupola and the wings protruding from each end as frightful and menacing. The elder's words pulsed through her head, making each step a thunderous beat.

"Death arrived. We wept until our eyes became a desert of emotion. Spirit left us. The moon betrayed us."

The yawning white porch echoed under her feet. She felt as though she were one of those little children, those free and wild young hearts, crushed beneath the weight of institution.

Here were the green tunnels. Halls with ceilings that soared above the child's head but pinned her down at the same time. Keshini trod down the echoing, slightly musty passageway. Worn linoleum held the imprint of tiny shoes. She imagined the old woman as a little girl. Her heart must have pounded like this: she must have been terrified. From open fields and forest to a burrow of harsh judgment. No more freedom, acceptance, natural communion. Do as I say. Speak as I do. Be as I am.

The archivist's room was quiet and orderly. Papers and books were stacked on a table. At first, Keshini worried that she shouldn't have arrived unannounced like this. Then the librarian opened her office door and smiled.

She was a matronly woman, round and soft, with a dark cloud of curls and kind hazel eyes. There was something about her that exuded understanding.

"Can I help you?" she asked.

"Yes. I wanted to see if there are any records of the students who were here when it was a residential school."

"I'm Shirley," the archivist said.

"My name's...Keshini. I'm staying in Vryheid for the summer. For the powwow."

Though the woman's eyes creased slightly at the name, she said, "Welcome, Keshini. I'm glad you came. I was doing some boring paperwork. And to answer your question, we have lots of records. In fact, I have some of them out on that table." She gestured to a stack nearby. "I've compiled the information for someone who's researching a novel. Have a seat."

They sat in front of the papers and books. Shirley selected a tall green ledger-style volume.

"What piqued your interest in the residential school?"

"I met a lady in Vryheid. I think she went here."

Shirley nodded. "The residential school system is one of the most shameful episodes of our country's past. It's hard to believe that the people in charge - government bureaucrats, politicians, educators, the churches - could actually think it was a good thing to do. They wanted to squash the native sensibility. Turn them into white people basically. What better way to rip apart a culture than to start with the children?"

She opened the ledger. "I think I know the lady from Vryheid whom you have been lucky enough to meet. Let me show you something."

And just like that, Keshini learned the old woman's history and felt the impact of prejudice, mistreatment and abuse.

"Death arrived. They left the world under the weight of white. They left without knowing who they were. Spirits left before the bodies did. Eyes vacant. Look at your eyes, Keshini. No one looks out from them.

"How light in my arms. How pale and small. The birds comfort them. Eyes that don't see have the sky before them. Stars at night, sun in the day."

***

Inside the circle of evergreens and lush bushes, the air was cool and quiet. Emily and William stared at the apparition before them. Built of sturdy logs, bark blackened by time. Surrounded by a riotous array of colorful flowers and weeds, yellow, red, pink, purple, orange, the cabin looked cared-for and welcoming despite its guarded nature.

They looked at each other, uncertain, feeling the silence like an invisible wall. At that moment a sob burst forth from behind the door. They both recognized instantly the voice that carried such grief.

The door was unlocked. They careened into a tiny square room, mottled with sparse sunlight that seeped through trees and leaves and curtained windows. In one corner stood a miniature kitchen with a table and two chairs. In the middle of the room, two ancient rocking chairs faced a ragged carpet and a pot-bellied stove. A single bed was shoved up against the far wall.

On the bed was their daughter Cate. She wept over a prone figure who lay unnaturally still. Long grey hair spilled over the girl's lap.

Emily and William knelt on the floor in front of her, speechless with shock. Cate gazed at her parents with a tear-streaked face, her eyes infinitely sad. She reached out and grasped a hand of each of them.

"This is Dr. Kathy Tyendinaga." Cate's words were formal and stilted but her voice shook. "Her real name was Kathyayini but they shortened it to sound more English. It meant goddess of power. Last week she said she didn't feel her power any more. She was my friend. I called her Akhso, which means grandmother. She's gone now."

"Oh, sweetheart." Emily could barely stand the grief infused in her daughter's statements, even though her head swam with questions and bewilderment. Instead of asking anything, she reached out and smoothed the old woman's hair away from her cold face. Gently she closed the vacant eyes.

Cate watched her mother's movements with gratitude.

"Do you want to stand up now?" William asked.

"Yes." Cate reached up to Emily as though she were a toddler.

William carefully moved the body as his wife gathered their little girl in her arms. Lifting Cate over to one of the rocking chairs, she cuddled her daughter as the tears flowed. Behind them, William covered the elder reverently with a blanket. He took care to place Kathyayini's long hair over her shoulders. Folded her hands in a prayer on her chest.

"Is this where you've been coming all summer?"

Cate turned her head up toward Emily's, content to stay stretched out in the rocking chair in her mother's arms.

"Yes. I'm sorry I didn't tell you, Mem. Kathyayini was so private. She never wanted me to tell anyone where she was."

Emily nodded. William sat in the chair next to them.

"Your mom wouldn't have told anyone," he said quietly. "You would have saved her and the rest of us a lot of worry."

Cate moved to the floor, sitting cross-legged on the ragged carpet in front of her parents. "I know. You're right. I got caught up in the secrecy and I didn't think."

"It's OK to have secrets, honey. We don't have to know everything all the time. But when it comes to your safety, it's better to let us know. And we want to reassure you that you can tell us anything. Don't be afraid to share your feelings or ideas. Ever."

Again their daughter nodded her lovely strawberry-blonde head.

"I'll remember, I promise. From now on."

"Can you tell us about Kathyayini now? We'll have to go to town soon and report her death."

"I met her on the path one day when I was out sketching. She liked my pictures. We started to talk and to meet often. She told me stories. All about her life and her sister and brother. They were taken to live in the residential school in Brantford. When I saw the skeletons at the church, I knew I had to tell her."

Emily and William waited as the child struggled through fresh grief.

"Later this summer, she began to wander in her mind. But she wouldn't get any help. She didn't want to live much longer. She said she was already ninety and she missed her family too much. I did some research at the Brantford museum. Kathyayini was a doctor of philosophy. As Dr. Kathy Tyler, she taught full time at the university. When she got old, she moved to her cabin to be near her sister and brother."

Cate looked up with red and swollen eyes.

"Keshini and Akash died and were buried at the residential school. The archivist told me that the same year, ten children died with no explanation. They just dumped their bodies in a plot of land next to the building. Even their parents, if they were still alive, wouldn't have been told."

Emily gasped. "That's awful."

"Disgusting," William agreed. "Sometimes people suck."

A glimmer of a smile played over Cate's lips. It was a phrase Carly had been told not to use in polite company. It seemed pretty apt just then.

"Big time," she said. "When Kathyayini retired and started to get dementia, she decided she would move Keshini and Akash to the church. The village had recently burned down and no one went near the place. So she dug up their remains and moved them."

"Wow. I wonder how she managed that."

"I don't know. She didn't give me any details. But it must've been hard and she was around sixty when she did it."

For Emily, sixty wasn't old, but clearly Cate thought someone of that age almost incapable of such a physical feat.

"Kathyayini said she wanted her brother and sister to have fresh air and be surrounded by the forest again. She didn't think anyone would ever find them."

"If it hadn't been for the earthquake, maybe they wouldn't have," William said. "The church was renovated a few years ago and they didn't find the skeletons."

"I don't know where she put them but it must've been up inside the steeple, I guess. They would've been just bones by then. When I got here to tell her about the earthquake, she was too sick to hear. Or talk. I sat with her for a minute and then…her spirit left."

"We have to tell the Brant police. Do you want to stay here and I'll go?" William stood up.

"That would be great," Emily said. "Cate and I will stay with Kathyayini. Maybe we can plan a ceremony for her and Keshini and Akash."

When William left, Cate and Emily sat side by side in the old rockers, holding hands, listening to the birds and squirrels chatter at one another in the trees.

"Sometimes she called me Keshini," Cate said finally. "I think she got mixed up and thought I was her sister. That name means beautiful hair."

"Perhaps she wasn't so mixed up, my love. You have beautiful hair and you must have given Kathyayini a lot of love in these last few weeks. Sister or granddaughter, you were a source of joy for her."

So it was that the day before the Burchill residents were to return home, they gathered once more with the people of Vryheid, Burford and Brantford. Although the church was still a construction site, the track had been cleared of debris. The new flagpole was ready to receive its memorial pennant. The dancers and musicians played out a more solemn chant than previously, as there was an addition to the ceremony. An oak casket, containing the remains of Kathyayini, Keshini and Akash Tyandaga, shone in the bright sunshine.

Chief Dan Mahdahbee opened the celebration with a prayer. "Oh, Great Spirit, Creator of all things: animals, trees, grass, berries. Help us. Be kind to us. Let us be happy on earth. Let us lead our children to a good life and old age. To see green trees, green grass, flowers and berries. Allow us all to meet again in joy and love. Oh, Great Spirit, we ask this of you."

As the flag was lifted above their heads, the shaman of the local band spoke of its meaning. "The leaves of the trees are resplendent with colour, like the strands of humans throughout the world, like the hidden corners of our magnificent earth."

The emblem was beautiful, rich with earth colours and symbols, stunning from afar and mesmerizing up close. Next to it flew the Mohawk flag of peace, the wagon wheel insignia, a symbol of resistance to slavery, and the red and white maple leaf of Canada. Four sentries celebrated the courage and strength of the human spirit, of goodness, while reminding its people to be vigilant against evil. The crowd cheered with appreciation and awe.

The moment Cate stood at the podium, Emily began to weep. Her tears were part grief for this girl, this young woman, who had suffered a depth of tragedy and trauma that should never have happened to anyone. Catherine had not only survived, she had shown that she was capable of giving solace to someone else's heartbreak. Emily's tears were part joy, too. This was her daughter, not from birth but from the heart. As a mother she was bursting with pride, hope and love. She let her tears flow, quiet and unashamed.

Cate's voice was clear and strong in the microphone. Hushed and attentive, the crowd reacted to every statement with: *Amen, Ethonaiawen, please God, Yeho, blessings, so be it.*

"As a member of the white race whose ancestors came to Canada years ago, I am both ashamed and proud. There were those who meant well and did well. The flags of Vryheid give testimony to their goodness. There were those who meant well but did not do well. They were the forces behind the evil of residential schools.

"Kathyayini, Keshini and Akash Tyandaga were victims of this terrible wrongdoing. No apology or restitution can repay Keshini and Akash, for they lost their young lives long ago. For Kathyayini, I was lucky enough to be here at the right time. I told her I was sorry. I told her that her life was not in vain.

"For although Dr. Tyler thought she sold out to the system that spawned such abuse and error, she was wrong. She started courses at the university in Hamilton that made the foundation for aboriginal studies today. This amazing woman was brilliant and highly respected. This means that her Mohawk philosophy, her sense of the environment and love for people and animals, have become a part of everyone who heard her speeches and lectures, read her books and course outlines, and learned from her. Let us pray that her legacy will go forward for a long time."

During the applause, Cate, Emily and Carly moved behind the coffin. William, along with Chief Dan and various Vryheid descendents, carried the remains to a plot next to the church. As they lowered the casket, the crowd threw flowers and seeds into the ground.

"Thank you, Dr. Kathyayini Tyandaga," Cate said.

With that, the crowd turned and walked toward the village and the feast they had planned: white, brown, black, tall, short, small and big, side by side by side.

Author's Note: *The Three R's* is an amalgam of the characters and setting of my *Emily Taylor Mysteries* and my standalone novel, *Sweet Karoline*. My research into Joseph Brant and the history of slaves and native people for *Sweet Karoline* led me to the former residential school in Brantford. There really is a librarian (not Shirley) whose knowledge, sensitivity and understanding were the inspiration for this story. Native children did die and were buried on that site. I still weep for them. Only a few generations apart, a shift in birthplace, and those children could have been my own.

About Catherine Astolfo

The *Emily Taylor Mystery series* features an elementary school principal who becomes a reluctant sleuth.

Book One, *The Bridgeman*, was honoured with a Brampton Arts Award. Books Two to Four followed from 2006 to 2010, to rave reviews. *Seventh Fire* completed the *Emily Taylor Mystery series* (at least for now!).

In 2011, Catherine signed with Imajin Books for the e-book and paperback versions of the Emily Taylor series (Imajin Books). Catherine won the prestigious Arthur Ellis Award for Best Crime Short Story in Canada, for *What Kelly Did*.

Catherine is a Past President of Crime Writers of Canada (CWC) and is a member of Sisters in Crime (Toronto). In 2012, she was awarded the Derrick Murdoch Award for outstanding service to CWC. *Sweet Karoline*, (Imajin Books) is now available.

Connect with Catherine at:
http://www.catherineastolfo.com/
FaceBook: Cathy Astolfo
Twitter: @CathyAstolfo
www.mesdamesofmayhem.com

Saving Bessie's Worms

by Lynne Murphy

Everyone who knew Bessie Bottomly thought she was invincible. So when she fell and fractured her leg at Cottonwoods Condo one winter day, all her friends were stunned.

It was Roger Trombley, the concierge, who found her, lying in pain in the hallway outside the plant room. Bessie insisted she was all right but when Roger tried to help her up, she screamed. That was when he called for an ambulance and summoned her best friend, Charlotte Manners. Charlotte rushed down and followed the ambulance to the hospital in her car.

There Bessie was diagnosed with a broken femur and told she would need surgery to pin the bone. Charlotte waited till Bessie's son arrived at the hospital and then drove back to the condo to report. She gathered most of the other ladies who made up the exercise group, the garden committee, the bridge and euchre clubs, in her apartment and made coffee.

"I can't believe Bessie has osteoporosis," Charlotte told them. "The doctor said that it's quite severe. Probably she didn't fall and break the bone. It just snapped and caused her to fall."

"Bessie is so tall and she always walks so straight," Maisie said. "Now if it was me…"

Maisie had never reached the dignity of five feet even at her tallest. With age she had shrunk until she resembled a garden ornament, an illusion that was increased by her habit of wearing hats with pompoms, and little pointed boots.

"She's going to have surgery tomorrow, if they can fit her in. Then she'll be in hospital for a week or so before she goes to rehab," Charlotte said. She had been a registered nurse and was still the group's authority on medical matters. "We'll organize visitors as soon as she's through the operation."

This was standard procedure for the Sisterhood. When one of their members was in hospital or in rehab, they set up an informal visiting committee and someone tried to go see her every weekday. The patient's family was left to cope on weekends.

Bessie came through her surgery just fine, but she seemed subdued. She didn't boss the nurses around or tell her roommates what they should be doing to help them get better. The accident had affected her usual masterful way of dealing with life.

It was several days after the operation before she remembered her worms.

Bessie didn't have worms in the ordinary sense of the term. She raised worms to make compost for the condo's gardens. She had sent away for the starter kit and kept the worms in large plastic containers on her balcony in the summer and in the plant room in the winter. She had been coming away from feeding them when her femur snapped and she fell.

Olive was visiting when Bessie remembered.

"My worms," she shouted suddenly. "They haven't been fed for almost a week."

"Good Lord!" Olive said. She knew what that could mean.

"I blame all these painkillers I've been getting for making me forget about them. Olive, please take care of them while I'm in here. If it's not too late. The other girls will help."

Olive said, "Of course I'll look after them." She tried to interest Bessie in the latest condo news, but Bessie couldn't think about anything except her worms. Eventually Olive left, promising to feed them as soon as she got home. She had planned to go on downtown and be fitted for a new support bra, but Bessie's distress had left her feeling too antsy to enjoy shopping.

Bessie's worms were an asset to the condo. People saved food scraps to feed them, everything but meat and dairy products. They left the garbage in old coffee cans or plastic bags outside Bessie's door and she ground up the peelings, lettuce leaves and used tea bags to feed her worms. The coffee cans went back to their owners to be refilled. Over time the waste became rich compost.

When Olive got home, she went looking for anything that could be used as worm fodder. There wasn't much. She hadn't been saving her scraps since Bessie had been in hospital. Now she felt guilty for not thinking about the worms earlier, but she wasn't going to sacrifice a perfectly good bunch of broccoli just to feed them. Unfortunately, the ladies had already cleaned out Bessie's fridge—and eaten all the fruit and vegetables—or there would have been something there. She phoned Charlotte.

"I've got some orange peel and some cabbage leaves. I'll bring those down to you. But what happens if the worms don't get anything to eat? Do they just starve?"

"They eat each other," Olive said in her most ominous tones.

"That's horrible!"

"I guess at the end you have one very fat worm and then finally it dies. I have to get going, Charlotte. Can you bring me your garbage while I get the Phone Tree started? And I'll call Roger to help."

The Sisterhood didn't need Twitter. The Phone Tree worked just as well. Each lady phoned three other ladies and they phoned three more until everyone had been notified.

Operation Worm Rescue swung into gear. Soon all the ladies were busy blending fruit and vegetable scraps. But when Isobel and Olive met in the hallway, it didn't look like they had enough to satisfy a storage container of starving worms.

"I don't think that's going to do the little beggars for very long," Isobel said. "Should we throw in some other stuff? Frozen peas or something?"

"Let's go down to the plant room and give them this now," Olive said. "At least we can see if they're still alive. If they're dead already there's not much point to this, is there?"

In the elevator they met Maisie and Charlotte, also carrying plastic containers. It reminded Olive of something, but she couldn't think what.

"Gold and myrrh and frankincense," Maisie said suddenly and giggled. "It's just like a Christmas pageant in Sunday school."

Olive said, "Maisie!" She was a devoted church-goer and didn't like the idea of worms being compared to the baby Jesus.

Outside the door of the plant room they found at least ten ladies waiting and more were arriving from all directions.

"Holy doodle!" Isobel said. "It's like one of them flash mobs!"

Charlotte, who was more sensitive, found she had tears in her eyes.

Maisie opened the door and led the way to the plastic container where the worms lived. She lifted the lid and a very nasty smell filled the room.

"My goodness," Charlotte said, "It smells like…like…"

"It smells like shit," Isobel said. She was originally from Newfoundland and she believed in calling a spade a spade. The others had to agree. It smelled too awful to be called excrement. But there were live worms, wriggling about in the ordure, enjoying it.

While the ladies stood there absorbing the disgusting smell, the door of the plant room opened and a shrill voice said, "What is that 'orrible stink?"

The women turned, some of them still holding their noses, to face the French Woman. She had moved into the building some time ago, but everyone called her the French Woman because they were unable to pronounce her name. As Isobel said, with her raucous laugh, "You need to be able to roll your arrrrrss to do that." She was known as a chronic complainer and Roger had a visit from her almost every day.

"It's the worms," Olive said. "Bessie's worms. She's in hospital and we've come down to feed them."

"Merde!" the French Woman said. "She keeps worms here, in the plant room?"

"Just in the winter," Maisie said. "In the summer they live on her balcony."

"I am come down to water my plant. This stink is impossible. Surely this keeping worms is not allowed. There must be by-laws against it."

The ladies looked at each other. Could there by a by-law that forbade the keeping of worms?

"I will consult Roger," the French Woman said. She pronounced it Roh-jay. She turned about with a swirl of skirts and left the plant room.

Charlotte looked at the others and sighed. "I can see trouble coming. Well, let's get these little fellows fed and then we can start collecting more scraps. Don't anyone tell Bessie about this."

The French Woman's first action was to register a complaint with the management office. Management, who could also see trouble coming, told her they would raise the question of keeping worms at the next meeting of the Board. In the meantime, the French Woman started a petition.

There was great division in the condo over the question. The gardeners who used Bessie's compost were on her side. But there were those who thought a condo was no place to raise worms. "Suppose they got loose," one frightened woman said to Maisie. "They might get into the water supply."

This seemed unlikely to Maisie, but she didn't have any good argument to offer. And there were those who thought the whole thing was ridiculous and refused to have anything to do with the petition.

The next meeting of the Board was coming closer and the Sisterhood felt they had to come up with a solution quickly. The French Woman was not approachable. Francoise, who originally came from Quebec, tried speaking to her in French. The French Woman just gave her a cold stare and answered her snippily in English. Francoise was insulted. Olive asked Roger for ideas, but he had a healthy fear of the French Woman after his many run-ins with her.

"Let's just hope the Board can't find anything in the by-laws that stops people from keeping worms," he said.

"But if enough people sign the petition to have them removed, the Board will have to act," Olive said.

The situation was in this sort of limbo when Olive spotted the French Woman one morning in a local park, walking a dog. It wasn't the nearest park to the condo. Olive was only there because she had stayed overnight at her daughter's, baby sitting, and was walking home. The French Woman was behaving in a strange manner, looking over her shoulder every few minutes. Olive stepped behind a tree and watched the pair. The dog, about the size of a large mouse, eventually did what he was there to do and the French Woman scooped him up, tucked him in her enormous satchel and headed back to the parking lot. Olive followed her, dodging from tree to tree, and hoped she wouldn't be seen. This was very interesting. Dogs were not allowed in the condo, even as visitors.

The French Woman drove away. Olive was unable to follow her, but she hurried back to Cottonwoods as fast as she could go and called a meeting of the Sisterhood in her apartment.

"Could we kidnap the dog?" Maisie asked. "Like with Roo in the Pooh book?"

The others looked at her as if she had started speaking in tongues.

"You know. *Winnie the Pooh.* The other animals kidnap Roo and try to make Kanga do something or other? I was reading it just the other day."

"We don't have to kidnap the dog," Olive said. "You know it's strictly against the rules to keep a dog in the condo."

"I could have a guide dog because of my eyes," Maisie said.

"This dog was about six inches tall. You'd have to crawl around on your hands and knees to use him as a guide dog," Olive said.

Charlotte held up her hand. "Girls! I know what Olive is suggesting. We confront her and threaten to report her unless she withdraws her petition."

"Blackmail?" Isobel said. "Lord t'underin' Jasus, girls. I didn't know you had it in you."

Olive smiled primly. "I prefer to call it persuasion."

Charlotte nodded. "We make her an offer she can't refuse.

"Now what we have to do is follow her to the park the next time she goes out with that satchel. Then someone else has to lurk near her parking spot in the garage and wait for her to come back. Then someone else has to wait outside her apartment and confront her. It will take a lot of co-ordination."

"We could ask Roger for help," Isobel said. "He has those security cameras."

"We can't do that to Roger. If he knows there's a dog in the building, he has to report it or he might lose his job." Olive knew how things worked. She had once been on the Board.

"Can't we just confront her when she's going out some day?" Maisie asked.

The ladies thought about it, then Charlotte shook her head. "What if she didn't have the dog in her satchel that day and we asked to see inside it? She'd know then that we were on to her. No, we have to be sure she has him with her."

She took a notebook and pen from her purse.

"We'll need cell phones. Does everyone have one? My daughter made me get one for when I'm out in the car."

They all owned cell phones, although they all made excuses.

"My son insisted I get one." "My grandson gave me his old one." "The phone company talked me into taking a package that included one."

It was as if cell phones were slightly indecent.

"I'm the only one who has a car," Charlotte said. "I'll take the job of following her to the park."

"I wish I could follow her in a taxi," Maisie said. "I've always wanted to get into a taxi and say 'Follow that car.'"

"You can lurk in the garage. I think Francoise has the parking spot across from her. We'll ask to use her car as an observation post and you can hide out in it. The French Woman won't notice you in there because you're so small," Charlotte said.

Olive and Isobel were assigned to The Confrontation since the Sisterhood felt there should be two of them for that. The French Woman was petite, but she was younger than any of them and might turn nasty.

It took several precious days to get everything co-coordinated with cell phones in place and timing all set. They had observed that the French Woman took her satchel out with her every morning around nine o'clock and returned about an hour later. On Tuesday morning, when the ladies should have been at exercise class, they assembled and all the participants took up positions. The French Woman lived on the ground floor of the building so Olive and Isobel waited in the lobby to watch for her return. At nine thirty, Isobel's cell phone rang.

"That was Charlotte," she said breathlessly after switching off. "The perp and the dog were in the park and the perp is heading back."

"The perp?"

"That's what the cops call crooks on TV."

Ten minutes later the phone rang again. It was Maisie.

"Suspect has just parked car in garage. Leaving said vehicle with suspicious satchel. Over and out."

"I think this has gone to Maisie's head," Olive said.

The elevator door opened and the French Woman stepped out, her satchel over her arm. Olive and Isobel rose from the banquette in the lobby and followed her down the hall. When she reached her apartment door, they were right behind her.

"We'd like a word with you," Isobel said.

The French Woman jumped.

"Could we step inside?" Olive asked politely.

The French Woman turned her key with trembling hands. She opened the door and ushered them in.

"We want to talk to you about what you've got in the satchel," Isobel said.

The French Woman clutched her satchel very tightly. It let out a startled yip.

"Whatever you've got in there," Isobel said.

Without speaking, the French Woman set the satchel on the floor and opened it. A tiny, apricot coloured head peeked out. The ladies couldn't keep from saying, "God love him!" and, "The little darling!" But they pulled themselves together.

"You know dogs aren't allowed in the condo," Isobel said. "We should report you."

"I cannot give heem up, my leetle Coco," the French Woman said piteously. "He is like my own child."

"Then you know how Bessie feels about her worms," Isobel said, though privately she thought it would be a cold day in hell before anyone could get her to think of worms as children.

"We have come to make you an offer," Olive said. "We will not report Coco to the Board if you will withdraw your petition and your complaint."

The French Woman considered, then gave a very Gallic shrug. "I have no choice. I must accept your terms."

Isobel had a brief fantasy of holding out her hand to receive a sword.

"You can trust us to keep quiet," she said. "If someone reports Coco, it won't be any of us."

The visitors turned and left the apartment to report to their fellow combatants. In the lobby Maisie and Charlotte were waiting for them.

"It worked, but I feel kind of mean," Isobel said. "He is such a darling little dog."

The ladies were quiet for a moment, then Olive said, "Maisie, why don't you look into getting a guide dog?"

About Lynne Murphy

Lynne Murphy read her first mystery when she was about eight. It was *The Secret in the Old Well* by Carolyn Keene, and she has been addicted ever since.

She studied journalism at Carleton University and worked as a reporter on the now defunct *Ottawa Journal* and then as an editor for *CBC Radio News*. (It was in the sixties and Lynne was the first woman editor they ever hired.) It was there she learned to "write tight".

Lynne has sold articles through the years, but *The Troublemaker* in the Sisters in Crime anthology, *The Whole She-Bang,* is her first published work of fiction.

In 1992, Lynne helped found the Toronto Chapter of Sisters in Crime and is proud that it continues to thrive.

Her major indulgence is travel.

Connect with Lynne at:
www.mesdamesofmayhem.com

Judgmental

by Catherine Dunphy

Such a charming man. The way he bends so his blue eyes are level with yours. And, ooh, he listens attentively, as if he'd never before heard anyone say they liked his book—at least not as well as I just have. The smile—a blast of delight and dazzle—and the *pièce de résistance*, the voice. Low and sinewy, for me only.

But then he enters the library.

Perhaps I should explain how I, a proud librarian, came to be in the company of Sidney Somerville, a man whose collected works take up precisely thirteen centimetres of the second-from-the-bottom row of the Fiction-Literature section in the library where I work.

Although I'm not unhappy about it, I'm not responsible for the location of the Somerville *oeuvre* on a row well below eye level unless you're a dog (which we don't allow in the library). That is due entirely to the Dewey Decimal System, still beloved by many librarians, myself included. The limited space he occupies, however, is all his own doing. Or not doing. Sidney Somerville has written exactly one novel. We have the hardcover edition of *Falling Leaves*, the trade paperback and the new re-release from a small publisher with government grant money to spend.

One would think he'd be happy about this, but no, the author is—there is no other way to phrase this—pissed.

"I would never have come to this godforsaken spot had I known that my work was being denigrated in this manner," he thunders at me.

He glowers like Mr. Rochester before he fell for Jane, until I summon Jason, our part-timer, to move the books to the F section. That is all I am willing to do. After all I cannot change the order of the alphabet, which Somerville seems to expect.

It is still not enough for him. He pouts until Jason deftly places the *Falling Leaves* hardcover in the Recommended Reads section. All by itself. On the top shelf. Face out.

"Place of honour, right where it belongs, sir," he chirps.

Somerville tilts his oversized head at me as if to say, "You see? At least someone here appreciates my worth."

Jason is Mr. Mollify. Living with his grandmother, placating has become second nature to him.

Mrs. Justice Sanderson Taylor, doyenne of our town's leading book club, or as she prefers it to be known, reading salon, is also its richest citizen. She is accustomed to getting her way. A year ago she'd commanded me via a shaking, pleading intermediary to employ her grandson. Jason was holed up in her basement working on his internet start-up company selling monogrammed jockstraps. Mrs. Justice Sanderson Taylor was neither supportive nor amused.

I like Jason, even though his work clothes alternate between a Ramones and a Duck Dynasty T-shirt. I found a line in the budget that let me employ him a couple of mornings a week, and that got me an audience with Mrs. Justice Sanderson Taylor, as I anticipated. I was able to successfully put forward my case for her underwriting my dream—a Millartown Librarians' Ball, a glittering literary gathering of the wealthy, the influential, the cognoscenti. Everyone honouring books, libraries, and, ahem, the people who work in them.

I've been working on this since I came here five years ago. We librarians read and therefore know all; we read, recommend and ignite the passion for bespectacled boy wizards; we steer enough people to books to set trends; we change lives. Yes, change lives. Name one autobiography wherein the author doesn't reference a book—read as an adolescent, often while convalescing—that riveted and redirected him (yes, it's usually him). You can't.

Nor could Mrs. Justice Sanderson Taylor, who perhaps was thinking of the young man glued to his computer screen in her basement. She also agreed to fund my other idea—the Librarians' New Talent Award, with a not inconsiderable $5,000 for the winner.

Everything to do with the award has been first class until Somerville came along. Of course I know he is, at best, a minor talent. Had I any say in this, I would be now leading Julian Barnes, that beautiful man, away from our library and down the main street to our restored historic mill. Or Kate Atkinson, even though she gave up on Jackson Brodie and the mystery genre.

Instead I have Somerville by my side, letting me know he is peeved at the lack of a decent single malt scotch in his mini bar. He is greatly offended at not yet meeting Mrs. Justice Stephenson Taylor, whom, he understands, is the rich, powerful benefactor of the award and ergo should be eager to share his company. I stifle a sigh. Mrs. Justice Sanderson Taylor is reluctant to fraternize with writers, believing many to be unkempt, even unwashed. She made it clear she would meet the man only at the ceremony itself, before he hit the free bar and unleashed his inner boor.

More like bore, I now think. Although Somerville might pass her dress code. He is dressed age appropriately, if a tad foppishly, with his bespoke suit and polished shoes. But I really do think the pocket puff went out of fashion two decades ago, maybe more. And does it have to be lavender?

I pause before I open the door to the mill. It is the town's showpiece, its heart. Crafted in the mid-nineteenth century by Scottish stonemasons, it's been restored by a team of our local power brokers, or more accurately, their wives. Even with their best efforts though, funding ran out before they could reclaim the basement level. It's a gruesome, mute testament to the tougher times—and rotten working conditions—of a mill town like ours. In fact, I happen to know that it served as a prison for a couple of years. Somerville won't be seeing that. Nor will the two hundred guests due to arrive in a couple of hours.

We are having the Librarians' Ball in the mill. Tonight, this is where Somerville will announce the winner of the very first Librarians' New Talent Award. It marks the official opening of the restored mill, the first time the public will see the place. I lobbied hard to have the ball here. I watched the main level brought back to life and rejoiced. I don't mind that the basement hasn't been buffed and modernized. I think we should all remember what once was.

I push open the beautiful heavy oak doors, noting that Somerville offers me no help. I turn on the lights, revealing the room's gleaming wide-planked pine flooring, the old warmth of its stone walls, the dignity of its proportions and the original mill office counter repurposed as the head table.

Somerville stops. "This," he says with a wave of his hand, "is extraordinary."

I am showing him where he will stand, where the cameras will be, when I hear a gasp. I know who it is. Winona Fletcher, my assistant, is a computer genius, whose skills I have put to excellent use. Did I mention I am head librarian for the region with a passion for local history? Please don't picture a historian-librarian as someone who stuffs facial tissue up their sleeve. I am tall and trim and currently garbed—now that's a librarian's word—in a Donna Karan sheath and killer red heels.

And Winona is punk'd out today with a new pair of chartreuse cat's-eye glasses that set off her ripped black tank. Several tie-dyed scarves round her neck clash very deliberately with her authentic 1950s poodle skirt.

She is as breathless as Marilyn Monroe, a heroine of hers. "Oh, Mr. Somerville, you are here. Really here."

She clasps her hands over her chest, which is heaving like a Harlequin grey-eyed governess swept into the ardent arms of her heretofore flinty-eyed employer. (Our readers are not fond of the modern romance novel in which the investment-dealing heroine has enthusiastic and drunken sex by Chapter Two.)

To his credit, Somerville's slack-jawed reaction to this vision—did I mention that Winona has a tattoo sleeve of Jane Austen heroines on her left arm? And should lose, maybe, eighty pounds?—is swiftly replaced by a countenance of rueful warmth.

"I am indeed. And delighted, if I may say so, to be in your beautiful part of the world."

His eyes twinkle on cue.

Winona appears to be swooning at his approval. "When you agreed to head our judging committee, I thought my heart would stop," she gushes.

Another thespian wave of that blasted hand. "My pleasure," Somerville replies. "I was happy you agreed with me that if I were to judge, you didn't need a committee."

"Oh, no," Winona breathes. "You were more than enough."

She beams at him. I stare at her. My assistant has had a personality transplant.

"I was the one who sent you the entries." My God, she is actually simpering. And I thought that only happened in books. "But when you said you would be coming to the ceremony..."

For the sake of my sanity, I interrupt. "A Somerville returning to Somerville. The town's legacy comes full circle."

And there, dear reader, you have it. Our hook. The *why* and *how* we lured Somerville the man to Somerville the town. Our persuasive powers were augmented by a first-class ticket to Toronto, a waiting limo that whisked him to the best suite in our finest—and only—four-star hotel plus a thousand bucks for his trouble. Courtesy of Mrs. Justice Sanderson Taylor who will be in attendance tonight to accept our gratitude, accompanied by her oxygen tank.

It was Winona who found the Somerville connection. Her fingers danced over the computer keys as she showed me that Sidney Somerville, the American man of (few) letters, was a descendant of Arthur Sidney Somerville, third and youngest son of the fifth Earl of Pitsworthy-Foxbridge. Arthur had been dispatched to the colonies where he soon required rescuing by his exasperated father. A series of adventures involving whiskey trading and imbibing landed the kid in the clink in Quebec City.

The Earl, who hated the French, decided to buy his son a village in Upper Canada, where at least they spoke the Queen's English or a version thereof. History records that what he actually bought was the village's only commercial concern: this very mill, owned and operated since its inception by the Millars, the town's founding family. When he arrived, Arthur, not one to let jail time dent his high self-regard, promptly turfed the previous owner and renamed the town. Thus Millartown, population 217, became Somerville, population 216.

I was intrigued and had Winona forward me any and all files pertaining to this time in our town's history. I spent hours in my office reading them while Winona composed a brilliant letter inviting Somerville to be a judge. It included an edited version of the life of his illustrious titled ancestor—and plenty of blue-inked links leading him to sites heralding minor British lordships.

My assistant could really write; I'd had no idea.

When I said as much, she brushed it off. When I persisted—I know good writing—Winona lost her temper for the first and only time. "For God's sake, judging is all he does these days," she snarled. "That, and overpriced memoir writing classes."

I retreated to our compelling archives of local history and left the care and feeding of Sidney Somerville to her. I communicated with him just the once, six weeks ago, inquiring, as civilly as possible, as to when he would so kindly be forwarding me the name of the winner. I had to personalize the award we would be presenting, I reminded him.

Two days later, he sent along the name of a young man from—where else?—Toronto. Three days after that, Winona burst into my office. Giving me no time to close the file I'd been reading, she screeched: "We got him. We got him."

When she told me Somerville was coming—in person!!—to present the award, I suppose I looked somewhat less than thrilled.

"Don't worry, Miss Mills," Winona said. "Jason and I have worked it all out. Mrs. Justice Sanderson Taylor is paying for it."

And now Winona is thrusting a pen and a copy of *Falling Leaves* at Somerville, as if he were Malcolm Gladwell, or even, for that matter, talented. "Please, I would be so honoured."

"Of course." Somerville preens, takes the pen, pauses, meets her eyes—meaningfully—and allows his lowest register to rumble forth. "To whom do I make this out?"

Pompous ass. To the woman who has written those masterful emails that got you here. To Winona, I want to say.

"To Frederika," Winona replies, ignoring my surprised glance. "Frederika Volkenheim."

Somerville laughs merrily. "That's a new one for me. Better spell it."

And after a moment, Winona does.

We watch as he inscribes the frontispiece of the book. I try to get Winona's attention, but she is spellbound by the man's ability to work a pen.

"Package for Mizzzzzzz Roseann Mills." Jason is dancing towards me, like a pillbox-hatted messenger in a classic comedy. He really is an antidote to his imperious grandmother. With deliberately arched eyebrows, he thrusts a large Canada Post express parcel at me.

It's the award, delivered in the nick of time to the library. My own design, crafted from ancient gleaming oak to resemble a book. The back cover opens to reveal a bronzed library envelope. The library card inside the envelope is parchment and bears the name of the winner.

I tear open the plastic puffy envelope. The award is unique; it's gorgeous, just as I'd hoped. It's a tribute to libraries and librarians everywhere. I clasp it to me.

"Lemme see it," says Jason.

Somerville takes in Jason's T-shirt and takes charge.

"Young man," he says peremptorily, thrusting aging shoulders back in a futile attempt to look down at Jason, who is a six-foot-six beanpole. "In two hours, you and the world will know the name contained therein. Until then, only I—the judge of this illustrious event—know the winner's identity. And it will remain so."

A click. Winona is recording this magnificent moment on her cell phone. Somerville smirks towards the camera—and delivers his coup de grace. "As for you, get yourself a day job, if anyone will have you."

I gape at the ridiculous, rude man. First of all, of course I know the identity of the winner. Secondly, he hasn't remembered Jason from the library. Thirdly, Somerville hasn't figured out his pedigree. The man's stupid; I'm suddenly thankful he hasn't inflicted a second book on the reading world.

But Jason, ever sunny, just grins and clicks his heels. "Will do."

Caterers are streaming in through the door bearing trays. Media have started to arrive, lugging cameras and boom mikes. I look at my watch. My God, Somerville is right. I've got two hours to get everything ready. Bar set up. Table seating arranged. Find the band. Get the sound system checked. Meet and wrangle the winner.

Winona reads my mind. "You need to get back to work. I'll take Mr. Somerville for a quick drink," she says, touching his arm. "Jason, go on home and get ready."

I leave, desperate to find the event planner, hoping he's on top of things. He is, and thankfully he has a safe place for the award. But it's more than ninety minutes before I look up from my clipboard of lists and catch my breath. Guests are arriving. There's an expectant buzz. I need to find Somerville.

I phone the hotel where the young receptionist tells me he and my assistant left the bar ages ago. I am nonplussed. And worried. "Did they say where they were going?"

"Maybe, like underground?" she says, sounding uncertain. "They were laughing about it. He was kind of leaning all over Winona."

I shake my head. Dear God, it can't be. Not Somerville. Not Winona.

I am standing in the middle of the old mill staring in despair at my cell phone when Jason appears, his regal white-haired grandmother on his arm, her contraption trailing. Jason has cleaned up, suited up and is attempting to lead her to a seat at the front of the hall. She is having none of it and is bearing down on me.

"Am I not to meet Mr. Somerville?" she demands. "Where is he?"

I seize the opportunity.

"I'll go get him." I hurry outside to the back where I collapse against the rough unrestored mill wall, Donna Karan dress be damned.

I am screwed. My Miss Mills persona is shredding as I panic. I try the deep breathing a yogi taught me years ago. I want the tranquillizers I got from the doctor in the next town last week just for times like this. But they are in my clutch, which is back in the hall where I can't go—not unless I come up with a damned good reason why Somerville has disappeared.

Then I hear Winona. She is crooning: her voice floats up through the rusting vent at my feet, accompanied by a furious clatter and clanging. "Frederika Volkenheim. Frederrrr-eee-ka. Remember it? That was her name. Fred-errr-eeee-ka."

She's in the basement.

I yank at the back door, take off my shoes and carefully climb down to the vile basement. A wild-eyed, dishevelled Somerville, hands tied behind his back and mouth covered tightly by several of Winona's tie-dyed scarves, is hurling himself against the bars of one of the historic cells. They're holding firm against his assault.

Winona whirls when she hears me.

"He didn't read a word. Not one word," she hisses.

She's gripping a ring of antique keys and a wrench one of the renovators must have left behind. She raises it menacingly. Somerville cowers and lifts pleading eyes toward me.

I ignore him.

"Talk to me," I say to my assistant.

She tells me she paid $3,500 for Somerville's online creative memoir course. Money she didn't have. But she figured it would be worth it if she could get his help to tell the story of Frederika Volkenheim, her father's great aunt, a daring explorer. Among the first westerners to traverse the Arabian desert and ride with the Bedouins, she was destined to be one of the century's great heroines. But the man she loved told her tales to T.E. Lawrence—yes, Lawrence of Arabia—who wove bits of them into the narrative that made him the stuff of myths and legend.

When Frederika approached publishers with her story, they laughed—and threatened to charge her with plagiarism if she didn't leave their offices immediately. She died broke, bitter and madder than hell, leaving a diary that neither her nephew nor his son—Winona's father—knew what to do with. But when Winona read it, she knew she must get Frederika's story published.

"I knew I could tell it well. I thought that if I could just get him to read it—" she stops, shoulders drooping, the wrench scraping against the earthen floor. Somerville flings himself again against the bars. I gesture at him to cut it out.

She sent in her writing every week, hoping he'd write back with criticisms, encouragement, anything. Instead she, and everyone else who paid money, received weekly boiler-plate writing tips from a do-not-reply email address. It didn't take long for Winona to figure out no one was reading her stuff.

I get it. "So you entered the memoir in the Librarians' New Talent Award contest. And Somerville didn't read it then either, did he?"

A miserable Winona nods. "He didn't even know her name. Frederika Volkenheim. He asked me to spell it."

Somerville is suddenly very still. I take a step towards him. "You didn't read any of the entries, did you? What did you do when I asked you for the winner? Pick the name of the guy from Toronto out of your hat?"

I reach through the bars and pull down his gag.

"Let me out. She's crazy. I can explain. It's not what you—"

I pluck the lavender puff from his pocket, shove it into his mouth, and pull his tie-dyed gag back up.

"I want you to listen. For once. Listen hard." I pace barefooted up and down in front of the cell gathering my thoughts.

"The last man locked up in this cell was Thomas Millar. He ran things in town until your illustrious ancestor arrived to claim his daddy's gift."

Somerville's groan is muffled by his gag. I like his obvious discomfort. I continue.

"Arthur Sidney Somerville decided the town needed to know Thomas was yesterday's man. He hogtied him, dragged him down the main street behind wild horses, and had him horsewhipped. When he threw him in jail—right here—he didn't bother to feed him much. Just the oats he would have given to his horses, a few sips of water."

I look at Somerville, also a bully and a cheat, and wonder at what DNA can transport through generations.

"I read that Thomas Millar scratched his initials on the wall over there." I point to the wall behind Somerville, who was now slumped like an abandoned puppet. "Thomas Millar spent twenty-seven nights in this dark and dank place. Long enough to lose some of his mind and all of his hope."

Somerville is not looking at me. But I am not finished.

"He died here. Because of a Somerville."

I stop. Winona's eyes are huge. I've known some of this story for five years, all of it for the past year. I've never told it before.

"So," she says slowly, "you're OK with him staying here?"

"Oh, I think he belongs here," I say.

We smile at each other.

"Yes, but, ladies, he can't stay." Jason walks up to Winona and puts an arm around her. "You OK, babe?" She nods, a happy flush rising up her neck to her cheeks.

Jason and Winona?

Somerville throws himself at the bars, grunting, sweat dripping into his gag and balling at his neck. I can see he is frantic, which makes me happy, but I also concede that Jason has a point. Sidney Somerville cannot remain locked up in the basement of the old Millartown mill. Still, it hurts to watch Jason take the keys from Winona and unlock the cell.

Somerville stumbles out. Jason rips off his gag, but does not, I notice, untie his hands. Somerville spits out his lavender puff. "I am calling the authorities and having you two arrested."

"Not so fast." There's a timbre, a new gravitas in Jason's voice. He is indeed a Sanderson Taylor. Even Somerville jerks to attention when Jason waves Winona's cell phone. "There's the matter of this video. Mrs. Justice Sanderson Taylor is the richest woman in the county, the widow of the chief justice, a force in these parts, Mr. Somerville. She is my grandmother, and when she learns that you insulted me and told me to get a day job, she will tear you to pieces." Jason grins. "Professionally speaking, of course."

Somerville wilts before us. That was his last hurrah. He's done.

Jason takes Somerville by the elbow. "Grandmother's driver is outside. He and I will escort you out of town and onto a plane. It's better for you that you don't meet my grandmother, believe me."

He pushes the man upstairs, although Somerville appears pretty eager to leave. Winona and I look at the empty jail cell and let out simultaneous sighs.

"Well," I say to her. "At least I don't think he will have the nerve to judge any more contests."

"No," she agrees, brightening at the thought.

From upstairs comes the sound of music. The band is playing. It's the signal that the awards ceremony is starting in a few minutes.

I will take over. Deliver Somerville's regrets. Perhaps I'll say he's been tied up at a previous engagement. Yes, that will do. I will have to give the guy from Toronto the award, but next year librarians will do the judging. They are fair and honest. Hell, they'll read 'em.

"Winona," I say. "Make sure you submit your story next year."

"Yes, Miss Mills," she says.

I straighten my dress, run fingers through my hair and slip my killer red heels back on. I'm ready.

"And Winona, I'm not Miss Mills. Not anymore. My real name is Roseann Millar. Thomas Millar, he was my great grandfather."

I'm the one who came back to reclaim Somerville. And after tonight, everyone is going to know it.

About Catherine Dunphy

A National Newspaper Award winner for feature writing, Catherine Dunphy was a staff writer at *The Toronto Star*, Canada's largest newspaper, for more than twenty-five years.

She is the author of *Morgentaler, A Difficult Hero*, which was nominated for the prestigious Governor General's Award in 1997. As well, she has written two books of young adult fiction related to the much-heralded Canadian television series, *Degrassi High*, which has been shown throughout the world.

She has also written screenplays for the Canadian television series, *Riverdale*, as well as created a four-part *CBC* radio mystery series called *Fallaway Ridge*. She currently writes for magazines and teaches print journalism and magazine writing at Ryerson University in Toronto.

Connect with Catherine at:
www.mmesdamesofmayhem.com

The Twin

by D. J. McIntosh

All the bright lights of heaven
will I make dark over thee,
and set darkness upon thy land.

Ezekiel 32:8

The cathedral had survived other wars. He hoped it would prove a sturdy sanctuary for the one that lay ahead. Warm wind came in great bursts and gusts. The priest raised his hand to stop the fine ochre-red dust, ever present in Baghdad, from blowing into his face.

A heap of refuse against the cathedral's front wall, stirred by the wind, caught his attention. Dirty plastic sheeting, the entrails of food packages, and bags stuffed with the possessions of some lost soul were bunched up in a pile.

The mound appeared to shift. Out of it emerged a gaunt tatter of a man. "Father," he called out, "could you wait?"

The man had a youthful voice but moved uncertainly, like an old person afraid of falling. A sweatshirt with the hood pulled up shadowed his face; baggy pants all but fell off his stick-thin frame. Probably sick, Father Tomas thought sadly, a common enough sight in many parts of the city. Still, the fellow seemed out of place here in the prosperous Karradah District. A student fallen on harsh times perhaps? Something unusual about the man caused a minute jolt of alarm, although the priest could not place exactly what that was.

He reached into his pocket for a few coins, hoping they would be enough to send the fellow on his way. "May I ask why you're here?"

"I feel better under the light," a pale finger pointed toward a fixture fastened to the wall. "I've been waiting to see a priest for hours, Father."

"And you are?"

"People call me Niko."

"Well, Niko. Let me go inside and see if I can find someone to help you."

The man grabbed the cleric's cassock with such force he almost tore the sleeve. "Please, I've already waited so long. I need to talk to a holy person."

The priest recoiled, pushing himself away from the man's sulphurous breath and grasping hands. He hurried up the steps and opened the heavy doors. Brushing his fingers with holy water, he made the sign of the cross and hurried down the central aisle. No footsteps followed in his wake.

The cathedral was empty. Any other time he would have welcomed solitude, but the strange man outside had upset him. The city was tense and unsettled, people deeply afraid. Who knew how this atmosphere might set off an already unbalanced individual?

Father Tomas took a seat in the front pew facing the wooden communion table and the simple altar draped with burgundy cloth. Below the crucifix, four tapers in tall candlesticks burned bright with flame. Together with candles in the wall sconces they cast a warm golden glow over the church interior. He touched the Assyrian cross he wore suspended from a chain of a precise length so it lay over his heart. He folded his hands in his lap, his feeling of serenity quickly restored by the calm tenor of the place. It reminded him of the gentle silence of being underwater.

What a contrast this simple place of worship was to his beloved Santa Maria Sopra Minerva, Rome's only Gothic church. So named because it was believed, erroneously, to have been built over an ancient temple dedicated to the Greek goddess.

His thoughts flew back to his many visits there: Bernini's statue of the elephant carrying an ancient Egyptian obelisk in the Piazza Della Minerva. Santa Maria's façade, so plain, one could easily pass it by without a second thought and miss the splendors waiting inside. Always upon entering the basilica, he would marvel at its beauty. The soaring nave patterned with tiny gilded stars, its vaulted ceiling of a blue so intense it seemed made of sapphire, the Maria chapel, the magnificent high altar. Fra Angelica's ornate tomb was there, and Michelangelo's majestic statue of Christ the Redeemer and Romano's Annunciation.

He closed his eyes and murmured a prayer for the safety of his two sisters, Maryam living with her family in Tikrit, and Leila working at al-Alwaiya, the children's hospital.

A bony finger prodded his shoulder, breaking his reverie. He whipped around nervously to see Niko in the pew behind him. There had been no warning as the man came through the doors. No muffled sound of footsteps. No telltale scrape as he took his seat.

"I want to make a confession," Niko said.

"I'm afraid confession isn't heard tonight." The priest scanned the seats, hoping for the reassurance of a few more warm bodies, but saw only yawning rows of empty pews. "I can't offer you confession anyway. This is not my parish."

"Please, Father. It would mean a great deal to me."

"What is your trouble?"

"I've hurt someone. The person closest to me."

"Well, you're to be commended for admitting that you've taken a wrong step. None of us goes through life without making mistakes. Whatever harm has been done I'm sure will be forgiven, if you summon the courage to ask."

"You don't understand. It's much worse than that."

Clearly the fellow was not to be put off. Perhaps the wiser path was to placate him. The cleric gestured toward a dark recess at the side of the cathedral, a small devotional area. "We can kneel together over there and pray."

An edge of fear resonated in Niko's voice. "No, I want to stay here and my prayers haven't worked."

"This is most unorthodox. Come and sit near me then. It will have to suffice."

Niko slid onto the front pew beside him, keeping his head bent so the priest could not easily see his face.

"How long has it been since your last confession?"

"This is my first."

"You're a member of the church?"

Niko nodded.

"This one?"

"Yes, Father."

"And you've received the Sacrament of Confirmation?"

"Of course."

"Then I can't imagine how it could be your first confession."

The man ignored this and repeated the ritual words. "Bless me Father for I have sinned."

The priest shifted further away on his seat and bowed his head. "Go on."

"Do you remember George Younis, the pianist?"

"Certainly. The family is well known in the city."

"I killed him."

Shock rippled through the priest's body. He strained to compose himself. Surely there must be some mistake. Perhaps this fellow was just desperate for attention. George Younis' death had been a great tragedy. A musical prodigy, he'd made a name for himself in America, but had fallen ill and died on his last visit home to Baghdad.

Niko smiled strangely to himself and said: "George had too great a hold over me. I wanted to be appreciated for myself, not always outshone by him. I assumed the riches and acclaim he received would come to me. So I planned a horrible act. Nothing has turned out right. Now I just feel cursed."

"I was told he died suddenly from a sickness." Father Tomas tried to recall the name of the disease, but his memory failed him. "An infection, something that caused a very high fever."

"Meningitis, is that what they said?"

"Yes, that's it. Meningitis. I can't believe his doctors would be wrong about that."

"They put George in a dark hospital room, shut all the window blinds and kept him absolutely quiet. Only his parents were allowed in. It gave me the time I needed, you see."

What was he suggesting? That he'd somehow gotten access to the hospital room and ended Younis' life?

The man seemed restless; his hands shook and he couldn't seem to keep them still. He'd rub his jaw and fiddle with the hem of his sweatshirt. His nerves were completely shot, Father Tomas thought. He probably hadn't eaten a decent meal for days.

Niko spoke again. "They made it impossible for me to get anywhere near George. At first I found that agonizing. It was the only time in our lives we'd been separated and it almost killed me. Then I realized the incredible opportunity it offered. I saw my chance and slipped away for good. The disease didn't destroy George. He knew I was never coming back and couldn't survive without me."

A mental case, certainly. Father Tomas relaxed a little. There had been no killing after all. Very gifted people like George Younis invited obsessions from all kinds of people. But how would the two of them even know each other? George was from a well-regarded family, his father a wealthy merchant, his mother a professor. They had a summer home on the Black Sea and a London apartment. It was difficult to imagine his path ever crossing with this poor ragtag fellow, let alone the two of them sharing any relationship.

Niko mumbled something then raised his voice. "George and I were never apart, but the spotlight always picked him out. His brilliance, his good looks, his musical genius. No one ever stopped to think my quiet presence and support were vital to him."

Who was this? A brother the family was ashamed of and kept hidden away? Possibly a twin? George had been on the short side and slim. In this respect the man resembled him. No, it seemed unlikely. The priest knew the family well enough. A housekeeper's child then? Someone who'd grown up alongside George and had persuaded himself they were on the same level? That made more sense.

"I felt compelled to copy him," Niko continued. "George liked to practice music in the evenings at home. As a little ritual, he would light the candelabra and let me sit beside him. I could not read music, you see, even though my memory was prodigious. Much better than his really. I could play just by mimicking the movement of his fingers. Or so I thought. But when I was alone and put my own hands on the keys, it turned out to be a total failure. He even took me with him across the ocean. To the jeweled school."

What was he talking about? Jeweled school? When the cleric realized what Niko meant, he had to stifle a laugh.

"You mean Juilliard."

"Yes. I went to school there with him."

This was plainly a fantasy. He'd blown what was, at best, a slight acquaintance far out of proportion. The bond existed only inside his head.

Niko reached into the pocket of his bulky sweatshirt and felt for something. Could he be carrying a weapon of some kind? Father Tomas felt a sudden thrust of fear. It was disconcerting not to be able to see the man's features. He wanted to get away and searched for the right words to end their conversation gracefully. "Such a gift as George had is rarely duplicated. We each possess capabilities God granted us, however humble. Better you should focus on your own talents rather than aim to be something you're not."

"You don't understand. I tried to strike out on my own, but George always pulled me back. It was like an invisible thread stitched us together."

"My son, I do sympathize. The grief of George's passing has affected you, more than most perhaps. I don't wonder at that, hearing how close the two of you were. But consider. The better part of your life is ahead. Don't give in to bitterness or regret. As to any mortal sin, you're blameless. I realize you're experiencing remorse, but that's a long way from actually having killed someone."

The tremor in Niko's hands spread to his whole body. He shouted at the priest. "You're still not listening to me. I need to be forgiven."

Father Tomas shuddered. The fellow was really disturbed. Nothing could be achieved by further talk. He rose quickly and moved away. Again the sense of something bizarre, almost alien about Niko struck him.

When his gaze drifted to the man's feet, the reality of who stood near him hit the priest like a shockwave. He experienced a frozen moment of indecision and then his thoughts clarified. He knew what he had to do. He walked up to the altar and extinguished the first taper, then the second.

As he reached for the third one, Niko said, "What are you doing?"

"If the power stations are destroyed, we'll have no lights. We're desperately short of candles as it is." The last flame sputtered out. He went over to a table holding votive candles in small blue glass receptacles, almost a third of them flickering with flames lit by parishioners. He put each one out with his fingers, wincing from the searing burn on his skin.

"Those are people's prayers. You can't do that," Niko cried.

"We have almost none left. They must be rationed, too."

The wall sconce candles were last. Father Tomas moved to the end of the side aisle and snuffed the first one out.

Niko ran toward him. "Don't touch another one. I know what you're trying to do."

"These are not normal times. We have to take precautions."

The entire central square of the nave was now in deep shadow, so Niko could not cross to the aisle on other side. The light along this aisle was rapidly dimming; soon, it would be gone. He could sense himself weakening. He thrust his hand inside his pocket and felt for the fat serrated steel blade of his knife.

Niko slipped out the cathedral doors, leaving the knife where it had clattered onto the floor beside the priest's body. He drifted along a ribbon of illumination spun by wide pools of light rippling out from shop windows and apartment buildings.

The bombardment of Baghdad that began early in the morning nourished and fortified him. He basked in the great incandescent, green phosphorus blooms bursting into the sky and the long flares cast from fires that burned for hours. Their powerful radiance far surpassed the weak light he usually had to make do with. Niko's body strengthened and he felt filled with energy.

Within a day, most power stations and transformers had blown up. The entire electrical grid collapsed. When the rain of bombs finally stopped, Baghdad returned to the state of a village in prehistory. A blanket of darkness fell over the great metropolis. With nothing left to sustain him, Niko faded to a translucent slip of grey and finally disappeared.

A shadow may live without his master, but he cannot survive without light.

About D.J. McIntosh

D.J. (Dorothy) McIntosh left her professional job to carve out a career as an author. It took almost ten years to research and write her novel, *The Witch of Babylon*, but it's now been released in North America and has sold in twenty countries around the world.

The novel was chosen by *Amazon.ca* as one of the best books of the year and by *CNN International* as one of six enduring historical thrillers along with notable writers like Agatha Christie, Umberto Eco and Dan Brown.

In her new novel, *The Book of Stolen Tales* (Penguin Canada 2013), the dark origins of famous fairy tales come to life.

Connect with Dorothy at:

The Witch of Babylon: www.babylontrilogy.com

Website: www.djmcintosh.com

her Amazon Author Page

FaceBook: Dorothy McIntosh

Twitter: @DJMcIntosh1

www.mmesdamesofmayhem.com

The Blue Angel Bar and Bolt-Hole

by Melodie Campbell

The weedy guy at the bar was starting to annoy me. He was alien for sure with that leathery brown skin, but most definitely a guy. Don't know why it is, but race doesn't seem to stop most males. If I had three eyes and no hair, they wouldn't care as long as the front rack was generous and came along with all the usual female apertures.

I could see Dalamar starting to steam in the corner, so it was time for me to step in.

"Umm...you might want to cool down now, as my boyfriend in the corner isn't looking too happy."

Calling Dalamar a 'boy' friend is a bit like calling the big bang a recent event. The fellow is built like a Talesian Warlord and has seen more battle than a decent man ought to remember.

He's pretty decent to me, though.

The tall alien swung around. Dalamar was on his feet and coming over. I leaned forward and said quickly, "What's your name, honey?"

The alien squeaked, "Tommas."

Dal was upon us. He had his dark look on, but I confused him with a smile. "Dal honey, have you met Tommas? He was just asking about you. Tommas, this is Dalamar the Paladin. You know. You must have seen the vids."

Tommas looked up and his brown face tried to smile, but the quivering marred it.

"You know what a Paladin is, hon? Well, in the old days, they would have been a special kind of knight, I figure. These days, they do dangerous jobs for hire. Dal here is the best."

Dal grinned, and it wasn't nice. Teeth were showing, but the eyes weren't smiling.

"You starting a zoo, Mel?"

I put on my stern face. "Now, be nice. Tommas has come a long way and he wants to be friendly." The sort of friendly he originally suggested was not available in this bar, but I've learned there are some things you don't need to expound upon with Dal.

I turned back to Tommas, but he was scooting out the half door.

"Well, would you look at that? No guts at all." I shook my head.

Dal laughed. "Smart, though. At least he has good taste." He reached over and rumpled my long brown curls with a big hand.

I smiled up at him. Dal was a fixture at the Blue Angel and that suited me fine. It isn't easy running a bar on your own when you're a female human on the edge of the known universe. All sorts of frontier types show up here thirsty, and some of them don't have civilized manners. Uncle Rog left me this little gold mine in his will. I wanted to do him proud. And money, it was for the making, if you didn't mind serving the oddest beings in the galaxy—and slapping away a few stray hands, paws or tentacles.

Dal is freelance and calls The Blue Angel home when he is between jobs. He has a little room upstairs close to mine. I don't mind that he gets jealous. Makes for grand reunions.

"You going to do that job?"

I saw him frown. He knew the job to which I referred. The dusky blonde had come with all the right equipment to snag Dal's attention. She was bad news, I just knew it. But I didn't tell Dal what to do. If there was coin or credits to be made, he had a right to make it.

He looked over and searched my face. "She's not my type, you know. I like curvy brunettes."

"Thanks for the reassurance. Not thinking of that." But I was. My turn to frown. "There's something about her that doesn't ring true. I'm worried, Dal, and about you. Something stinks about this."

"Escorting her to a new government job on Sirminor 3? It isn't dangerous. I've done this stuff before. Easy credits."

I shook my head. Government job, my size seven foot. She didn't work for any civil service. There was nothing civil about that gal at all.

"There's something not right about her. Sorry, Dal, just got this feeling."

Dal took my feelings seriously. After all, I came from a long line of gypsy fortune tellers. It made for an interesting sideline when business was slow.

"When are you meeting her?"

Dal looked at his wristband. "Just about now."

I watched the door. "Gone for how long?"

"The minimum, if I have my way. Two days there, two back and one over."

I shivered. Damn, but I was feeling creepy.

I turned from the front and made my way behind the bar. It was a slow part of the afternoon. Just one gentle Plantilian in the snug fast asleep, and a couple of old frontier prospectors quietly playing cards. Customers would be piling in later, after work. Jackson would come to relieve me soon, so I could have the night off. Sad that it would be a night alone.

The blonde was back. Nope, I really didn't like her. There's something about synthetic blondes, especially tall thin ones. The blouse was too tight, and if that rack was real, I'd eat a reptisaurus.

"So, ready to go, handsome?"

Did I mention the fake Dixie accent?

"Mel, have you met Regan? Regan—Mel. She owns the bar here."

Regan raised one eyebrow in disdain. "Charmed, I'm sure."

Just like a snake, I wanted to say. Instead, I nodded, friendly-like.

"We'll take the table over there, " Dal said. Putting space between us was a good idea.

I took a rag and swiped at the bar.

Ten minutes later Jackson arrived and Dal looked about ready to leave. I walked around the bar and went over to say goodbye. This is a dangerous part of the galaxy. You never know what's going to happen when people walk out of The Blue Angel, so I always make my feelings plain. Dal was waiting for a big hug.

"Now don't you go worrying about us," Blondie said. "We'll be just dandy, and I know a million games to pass the time."

I put on my sweetest smile. "Regan, you have a spot on your blouse. I have autocleaners in the washrooms, if you'd like to avail yourself."

She looked down. "Well, so I have. Back in a minute, y'all."

She sashayed down the hall, slim hips swinging this way and that. I watched her turn left into the washroom.

Dal was looking at me, not her. "You really don't like her."

"She sparks with snakes as far as I'm concerned."

He laughed, then pulled me into a sideways hug.

"When are you leaving?"

"About two hours. I need to get supplies then load up."

I nodded, went up on tippy-toes, and gave him a light kiss on the lips. "Be safe."

He tried to reach for me, but I slipped his grasp. I ran up the stairs without looking back.

Easy to sneak on board when Dal was out collecting supplies. I knew the code, of course. It was my birthday.

"Mel, long time, no sense." Roz is Dal's onboard computer.

"Hiya, hon. I'm planning a surprise for the boss. Mum's the word."

"I had records of your last surprise. The boss made me delete them."

"Just be quiet about me being here. And don't you dare make records of us, honey."

"That's what the boss said. About the records. As you say, mum it is."

I didn't bring much. Just my regular things…nothing fancy. A change of clothes and a few essentials. My ID was under the skin of my left forearm. Dal always brought plenty of food and water. So I parked myself in the head and waited. Good place—everyone goes to the bathroom before a big trip, right? No need to use the head for a while.

I heard them board and drop parcels on the floor. I could hear talking, and once Dal laughed, but it was muffled. There was a clank as the docking clamps let loose. I felt the puff of maneuvering jets, then we hit the drive in Dal's characteristic way that leaves your stomach on the floor. I opened the door a smidge to peek out.

Dal was at the controls and Regan sat in the co-pilot chair. My chair.

"So, straight to Sirminor 3? No sideline shopping trips to the outlet malls?"

I saw Regan leave her chair and circle behind Dal. "No need, my friend. We're not going far."

There was a weapon in her hand and it was aimed at Dal's head.

"What the —" Dal had turned to face her.

I can move fast when I need to. The stunner beam hit her in the back, turning her neurons inside out. She crumpled with an "Eeeeep!"

Dal stared at her, then at me. He was mad—fuming mad at letting Regan get the drop on him. He exhaled sharply. "You really don't like her."

"Not so much," I said, reaching down. With one motion, I pulled off the blonde wig.

"Wallen!" Dal cried out.

"Isn't that the son of the man you escorted to Minlon last month? The guy headed for sonic obliteration?" A civilized world would have wiped the felon's brain, then put him to cleaning toilets for the rest of his life. Minlon wasn't civilized. They sold vids of the execution to defray costs.

"The very. He nearly got me on Blandon last week. But how did you know, Mel? What gave it away?"

I wrinkled my nose. "She looked like a woman, but she didn't act like one. Not sure I can put it in words, but it was something about the way she looked at me. Predatory…like some men do. So I set her up. That spot on her blouse? I wanted to watch her go to the washroom."

Dal's weathered face was still puzzled.

"She went to the Men's, Dal! Acted on instinct like I thought she would."

"Son of a bitch."

"Probably was," I agreed. I went over to sit in my chair.

Dal picked up the still unconscious Wallen. "Buddy is going to walk home." He carried Wallen to the airlock. I heard it cycle and shivered. Dal came back alone. He looked at me and shrugged.

"He played with the big boys and lost."

I swallowed hard. "I know. I can never get used to it though."

Dal strode over and took me in his arms. "Stay that way, beautiful. But let me keep you safe next time."

"Did it work, Mel?" Roz's voice soared through the cabin.

"Yes, honey. He was surprised."

"Surprised! I almost got killed."

"That wasn't part of the surprise?"

"No, Roz."

"But don't worry," I piped up. "I have another surprise for him. And no making records this time."

Roz sniggered. She knew a lot more about the human condition than she let on.

Melodie Campbell

Mesdames of Mayhem

Watermelon Weekend

by Donna Carrick

My mother believed in the irrepressible power of love.

Some might have called her a romantic, but that wasn't the case. When it came to distinguishing between love and romance, she could not have cited the definitions. She wasn't able to manipulate semantics in that way.

But she knew the meaning of the word.

I was the eldest of four boys raised by Elizabeth "Bessie" Fender.

I appeared on the scene when she was nineteen. At four months pregnant, she married my father, John Fender, for whom I was named. Dad finished high school and enlisted in the Armed Forces to provide for us.

Eighteen months later, he was dead. The only mementos I have are a pair of pictures on my nightstand. There's one of him with my mother, laughing on my grandfather's porch, and another where he's in full uniform about to ship out to Cyprus.

Oh, and the story of how he died—that's mine as well, though I usually keep it to myself. There's nothing noble in the concept of friendly fire. When his Canadian peace-keeping unit was hit that day, he wasn't the only casualty. A couple of civvies went down, but they aren't listed by name in the letter Mom received.

That's another story, and not one I like to dwell on. I never knew Dad, but I have to give him credit. According to my mother, he was handsome and brave, and, like her, he believed in love.

Because I had no father, Grandpa did his best to step into the role. He taught me to fish and how to fix things. He wasn't a violent man. I don't believe I ever saw him angry, not really. Still, he took the time to talk to me about self defense, in the way I imagined my own father would have if he'd lived.

"I don't go for weapons," he said. "If your enemy is bigger and stronger than you are, he's going to take your knife and use it against you.

"If you must fight with a weapon, don't let go of it no matter what. Consider it an extension of your hand. And don't hesitate to use it."

I nodded as if I understood.

"And Johnny," he added, "never forget: It's always best to walk away from a fight. A real man doesn't have to prove himself."

In my childish mind, I knew he was wrong. A man did have to prove himself.

"If you find yourself in a situation where you have to fight, for God's sake, fight hard. If you knock a man down, make sure he stays down."

"Have you ever been in a fight, Grandpa?" I asked.

"Once or twice, son."

He smiled, pointing at the kitchen cupboard. "Go get me the Phillips screwdriver," he said. "That hinge is loose. I know your mother. She'll be nagging us if she sees it."

It was Friday morning more than twenty years ago, when I was twelve going on thirteen. I could hear my eight-year-old brother, Nicky, crashing around in the bathroom. He was supposed to be brushing his teeth, but it sounded more like he was dismantling the plumbing.

The twins, David and Dale, were five. They were good boys, self-sufficient, although they liked to follow Nicky around at times, to his annoyance.

David was the quiet one, content to be in a room with his family. Dale was more talkative, interested in what was going on around him.

Nicky, for the most part, was a sullen child. He didn't cause trouble, but I guess you could say he had a chip on his shoulder. He liked to be left alone. The only person he really related to was our mother.

That Friday morning more than twenty years ago, we were packing for a weekend at the cottage. Grandpa owned a place up in Muskoka. Mom had a key and a standing invitation to take us there any time she liked.

We spent many weekends at Grandpa's cottage. In the old days he used to come with us, doing all the things a father would do. He taught us to play baseball, hauling out his pride and joy: a collectable 1938 *Louisville Slugger* his father had bought him when he first joined Little League.

He used to kid us, saying we had to be "this tall" before he'd let us hold the bat.

He always relented, to our delight. That's what Grandpas are for.

By the time I was twelve, Grandpa wasn't well anymore, and he didn't come up too often. He still liked to know we were using the place, though.

Mom had recently started dating Phil, a thirty-something salesman who was employed by a drug manufacturing company. No one at the pharmacy where she worked knew they were seeing each other. She'd told us about Phil earlier that week, but warned us not to say a word to Grandpa, at least until she was sure it would work out.

Even though Mom was a knockout at thirty-one, a single mother of four boys doesn't get many romantic offers, so she was excited to be dating again.

It was to be our first weekend together with Phil. He seemed like a nice enough guy. I could tell Mom was hoping it would get serious.

"Remember," she confided, "let's not put any pressure on the relationship. It's our secret for now. Don't mention it to Grandpa, or anyone."

I nodded.

I was glad to see Mom happy.

Not so my brother, Nicky. He'd been in a foul mood all week.

"Come on," I said, tapping on the bathroom door. "I need in there. The twins are already in the van."

Nicky didn't answer. A moment later the door opened and he came out, deliberately bumping into me.

I tended to make allowances for my half-brother. According to Grandpa, who seldom had a hard word for anyone, Nicky's father was a "no-good womanizing bum gambler". Steve did time for petty theft and car-jacking. His brief marriage to my mother had ended badly.

A few years later she met Brayden, a handsome musician. He was a nice fellow who paid attention to me and Nicky, which most guys wouldn't do.

When the ultra-sound revealed Mom was carrying his twins, Brayden screwed off. We have no idea where he went. We haven't seen him since.

I think the twins have it worse than Nicky does. At least Nicky's father didn't disappear. It must really suck to be so low on the totem pole.

Mom said the responsibility was too much for Brayden.

I have my own opinion. There are men who face their duties—men like my father and Grandpa—and there are those who don't. It's as simple as that.

I seldom think of Brayden. When I do, I admit it's with a certain measure of disdain.

"Get your stuff," I said. "Tell Mom I'll be right there."

Nicky grabbed his bag and stomped down the stairs.

So that's how we ended up in Mom's minivan on a sunny Friday morning in July. Two adults, four boys and one big hairy dog—our golden retriever, Fanny.

Nicky's mood lifted once we were on our way. He and I played *Mario* on our Gameboys. Dale fell asleep and David worked on a word search.

"Where do you want to shop?" Phil asked.

We were in Barrie with still a long way to go.

"There's a Sobeys up ahead," Mom said. "Do you boys want anything in particular?"

"Watermelon," Nicky said, smiling at the thought.

"Yes, watermelon," I agreed.

"Watermelon it is!" Phil said.

David clapped his hands.

Phil grinned at us in the rear view mirror. I wasn't sure why Mom had let him drive. After all it was our car, and Mom was a good driver.

But he seemed to know his way around, at least so far.

"Do you boys want to come in?" Mom said.

"No, we'll be all right here," I said.

"OK. Keep an eye on your brothers. If the car gets too hot, open a door."

"I'll stay with the boys," Phil said.

As soon as Mom went into the store, Phil pushed his seat back and closed his eyes. It could be a tedious drive if you weren't used to it.

Mom was in the store about a half an hour. When she returned, Nicky let out a low whistle.

"Holy crap!" I said.

Mom had gone all out. The buggy was piled high with food.

Nicky and I helped load the groceries into the van.

At the bottom of the buggy were three big green watermelons.

I should mention, Grandpa's cottage has a dock where he kept his boat tied up. The water there is deep and not too full of reeds.

That's where we learned to swim, doing cannon-ball jumps into the cold lake on a hot day.

Some of my best memories involve munching on watermelon with my legs dangling over the edge of that dock.

So yes, we were happy to see the watermelon.

I caught Nicky's eye. He was smiling for a change.

David fell asleep north of Barrie. I lost interest in playing with the Gameboys. I'd recently been teaching myself to play chess, so I challenged Nicky to a duel.

He was a better sport than I was, losing without complaint.

Before we knew it, we could see Go Home Lake. Within twenty minutes we'd be at the cottage.

What could be more thrilling for a boy than arriving at a crystalline lake with hours of sunlight still ahead and nothing to do but run, swim and play?

We hurried to change into our trunks and headed for the dock.

"Keep an eye on your brothers," Mom said.

"I will."

"Dale has trouble climbing out of the water."

"I know."

"I'll bring down some watermelon in half an hour."

"Hooray!" the twins shouted.

That evening Mom surprised us with a rare treat—six huge steaks on the barbecue. We ate till our stomachs were distended: baked potatoes, sour cream and corn on the cob.

"Anyone want more watermelon?" Phil asked.

Without waiting for an answer, he went to fetch a large bowl from the fridge.

Nicky and I groaned at the sight of the juicy red melon. Still, we couldn't help ourselves.

"You boys will be awake peeing all night long," Mom laughed, reaching for a piece.

"Let's hope not." Phil winked at Mom.

She giggled.

I bit into another piece of melon.

Nicky and I washed the dishes while Mom and Phil set up the DVD player.

It wasn't easy finding movies we all liked. Nicky and I would watch just about anything, but the twins got frightened easily. Especially Dale.

Mom finally decided on *Mrs. Doubtfire*.

"Be careful with that knife," Mom said.

I glanced at Nicky, who was carrying the big carving knife toward the sink. It was slick with watermelon juice.

Worried he might hurt himself, I reached for it.

He turned the handle toward me and I dipped the knife into the soapy water, careful not to cut myself.

We have a rule in our house: only Mom and I are allowed to handle the sharp knives. Rather than drying it, Nicky left it standing in the rack.

"Who wants popcorn?" Mom asked.

"We do!" my brothers shouted.

It isn't easy keeping boys fed. Grandpa used to accuse us of having hollow legs.

"Where'd you put your dinner?" he would joke, watching us go back to the stove for seconds.

The movie was a lot of laughs. Even Nicky enjoyed it. By comparison with Steve and Brayden, Robin Williams as Mrs. Doubtfire looked like some kind of Super-Dad.

The northern air was weighing on us, so after the movie Mom ordered us to brush our teeth and get to bed. Nicky and I shared a room near the kitchen, closest to the bathroom. Fanny usually slept on the floor between our single beds. David and Dale had bunk beds in the middle room. The third small room off the living room, farthest from the kitchen, was Grandpa's.

Mom had the master bedroom off the other side of the living room. The cottage had been designed by Grandpa back when Grandma was alive. The big room had belonged to them in those days, but Grandpa seldom came up anymore. When he did, he was happy to use the little room.

Being the oldest, I sometimes stayed up late watching movies with Mom, but it was obvious she wanted private time with Phil, so I didn't argue. Besides I was tired, and Nicky's mood was getting dicey.

I lay awake, listening to adult chatter in the other room. The sound was alien to me, but not unpleasant. Mom and Phil kept the TV volume low. Nicky was asleep in no time and I followed not long after, seduced by the honest fatigue of a day spent in the sunshine.

I don't know what woke me. Maybe it was some minor twitch of Nicky's or maybe Fanny rolled over on the floor. Our dog wasn't much of a talker. When she needed attention, she would give me a look. I don't think I ever heard her whine, and I could count the times she'd barked on one hand.

For whatever reason, I found myself suddenly awake, long after everyone else had gone to sleep.

Nicky had a tendency to get cranky if he didn't get his ten hours, so I crept silently out of bed to the kitchen to check the time.

The clock on the stove said 2:15 am.

I turned toward the bathroom and, as I did, I heard a whisper coming from the twins' room.

I thought I must be imagining it—there was no way either David or Dale would be awake at that hour. I was about to dismiss it when there it was again, the unmistakeable sound of a whisper coming from the middle bedroom.

David normally slept on the top bunk, being the braver of the two, and Dale was on the bottom.

Not sure of what I'd heard, and not wanting to wake them, I tiptoed to the doorway and peeked inside.

The twins had a nightlight, a plastic cartoon image, plugged into the outlet near the baseboard. By its light, and to my shock, I saw Phil stretched out on the bottom bunk beside my little brother.

I couldn't see his hands.

Dale saw me before Phil did. My brother's eyes were frightened, and there were tears glistening in the faint light.

Innocent me—I had no idea what was going on. But it didn't look right.

"Dale, are you sick?" I asked.

Phil stood, knocking his head on the top bunk and waking David.

"Dale was crying," he answered, too quickly. "I came to check on him."

"I'll get Mom."

"No need. Everything's all right now."

Dale still hadn't said a word.

"Was it your stomach?" I asked. Dale was sometimes prone to gas, which made him whiney.

He shook his head.

"What was it?" I insisted.

"I want to sleep with you and Nicky," he said.

"Me too," David chimed in.

Something wasn't right. I glanced at Phil and was not reassured by what I saw in his eyes. He was wearing a guilty look, the kind Nicky wore when we caught him red-handed eating the last of the cookies.

"I'll get Mom," I repeated.

Phil grabbed my shoulder as I turned.

"I said there's no need to wake your mother. Everything's all right now."

I have a real thing about being touched by strangers. The only man I'd ever admired and felt loved by was my Grandpa, and he wasn't the touchy-feely sort. He was far more likely to hand me a tool and let me work beside him. That was how we expressed our affection.

I shook Phil's hand off, probably with more force than I intended.

"Hey there," he said. "Just wait a minute."

"Leave me alone."

"What's going on?" I heard my mother's sleepy voice calling from the master bedroom. "Is everyone all right? I knew someone would have trouble sleeping after all that watermelon." She approached the twins' bedroom, pulling her robe over her shoulders.

"Everything's all right," Phil said. "I got up to use the bathroom and heard Dale crying. I came to check on him."

"I want my Mommy," Dale said, becoming hysterical at the sound of our mother's voice.

"There, there, baby. It's all right. Mommy's here now."

"Stay with me, Mommy."

"Stay with me," David repeated Dale's request, minus the tears.

"Is your tummy OK?"

Dale nodded.

"Do you need to use the bathroom?"

He shook his head.

"Do you have a headache?"

Again, the head shake.

"I think you've had a nightmare, sweetheart," she said, hugging my brother. "You close your eyes now and get back to sleep."

"It wasn't a nightmare, Mommy. It was Phil. He scared me."

My stomach tightened.

By now, Nicky was awake as well. He turned on the light and stood in the kitchen near the counter, a wary look on his face. Fanny was at his side.

"Phil was checking on you, dear," Mom said to Dale. "There's nothing to be afraid of."

"He hurt me. I want to sleep with John and Nicky."

Mom let go of Dale and stood, her full height falling short of Phil's by nearly a foot.

"What do you mean, Dale? How did Phil hurt you?"

"He wouldn't leave me alone." Dale began to wail uncontrollably. It was obvious we weren't going to get anything coherent out of him.

"What did you do?" Mom said to Phil, her voice cold in a way I'd never heard before.

"Oh, for Christ's sake, Bessie, the boy had a bad dream. I was checking on him. You baby them all too much."

"Mom," I said, reluctant to interfere, but unable to remain silent, "I saw Phil. He was under the covers with Dale. Dale was crying."

"What do you mean, under the covers?"

I looked at my feet. My vocabulary would not allow me to elaborate.

"Go." My mother pointed at the doorway, her eyes fastened on Phil's face. "Get your clothes on and get out."

"Where can I go?" Phil said. "We only brought your car."

"You can sleep in the van for tonight. In the morning, we'll call you a cab, and you can catch a bus in town."

"This is ridiculous!" he shouted. "I didn't do anything wrong."

"I don't know whether you did or didn't," Mom said, "but I want you out of my house. Do I need to call the police?"

I edged closer to the phone.

"Police?" Phil said, stepping towards our mother. "Are you threatening me?"

Fanny barked—only once. It was such an unusual sound I couldn't help but jump.

Nicky's shoulders stiffened. He slid closer to the dish rack. He caught my eye, and I knew what he was thinking.

Silently, I shook my head. I remembered my grandfather saying a weapon is only as good as the person holding it. If your enemy is bigger and stronger, he will likely take it and use it against you.

It was always better, according to Grandpa, to simply run, and if you couldn't run, then use your brain.

"Let's all settle down," I said in what I hoped was a smooth voice. "Come on, Dale. You've had a bad dream. You and David can sleep with me and Nicky tonight."

In my mind's eye, I saw the privacy latch my grandfather had attached to our bedroom door. "A boy your age needs to be able to lock the door every now and again," he said. I figured once the boys were in our room, we could lock it. If necessary, we could use my phone to call the cops.

Phil had other plans.

"Settle down?" he mimicked. "Who the hell do you think you're talking to?" Phil pushed Mom out of the bedroom. She hit her head on the door frame and fell onto the living room floor.

Fanny leapt forward, placing her body between Phil and our mother. Her efforts won her a kick in the ribs. She yelped, but did not move.

"That's enough," I said.

Nicky took another step toward the kitchen counter.

David scrambled down from the top bunk and ran to our mother.

"You little shit," Phil snarled in my direction, his congenial mask now long gone. "I could kill the lot of you and no one would even know I was here."

Dale let out a fresh howl.

"You hear me? I could start with Dale here, snap him in half with one hand and keep on going till I put every one of you miserable bastards down."

Phil reached for Dale, pulling him from the bottom bunk. He dug his fingers into Dale's fragile shoulder and pulled him past our mother into the living room.

"What's with this brat?" he said. "Doesn't he ever stop whining?"

He lifted Dale into the air and shook him, yelling, "Shut the fuck up."

Dale held his breath, doing his best not to cry.

Mom stood up.

"Please, Phil," she said, in her most reasonable Mom voice, "let's get some sleep. We're wound up. It's probably the watermelon."

"You stupid cow," Phil sneered, still holding Dale. "You think you're going to call the cops on me? A desperate bitch like you with your snivelling litter? Who else would have you?"

Nicky's hand moved quickly and quietly, lifting the knife from the dish rack. I don't think Phil noticed.

"I'm sorry, Phil," Mom said, remaining calm. "I didn't mean it. Let's go to bed. We can sort it out in the morning." She pushed David toward me with one hand. I grabbed him and shoved him behind me, into the kitchen.

Mom stepped towards Phil and Dale, nudging Fanny out of the way. She had to diffuse the situation before it got any more dangerous. She caught my eye. I knew she was counting on me to take care of the boys, get them to safety down the road, once she convinced Phil to join her back in bed.

Then, as if changing her mind, she suddenly stepped past Phil, heading toward Grandpa's room.

"What are you doing?" Phil shouted.

Mom didn't answer. She didn't have to. I knew what she was up to.

Grandpa always said a weapon was only as good as the person holding it. He didn't own a gun. He always said a determined criminal could overpower an honest man every time. A lethal weapon like a gun could be taken and used against you.

That didn't mean we shouldn't defend ourselves.

Nicky stepped past David and stood beside me, holding the large kitchen knife. For a second I thought he meant to pass it to me. After all, I was bigger and stronger.

When it came right down to it, though, he was probably tougher than I was. Squaring his shoulders, he prepared for battle.

"You've got to be kidding," Phil said. He looked at the knife in Nicky's hand. Holding Dale in front of him, he said, "I could snap your brother's neck like a twig. Is that what you want?"

"Nicky," I said, "give me the knife."

Reluctantly Nicky stepped back, handing me the weapon.

"That's more like it," Phil said. "Now, you boys get on the floor. Face down, side by side."

Nicky and I stood together, neither of us moving. I could hear David whimpering behind us, but I couldn't take my eyes off Phil long enough to check on him.

Nicky saw Mom come out of Grandpa's bedroom. When he realized what she meant to do, I could feel his energy change.

She had the advantage of surprise. With Phil focused on Nicky, me and the knife, she was able to bring up the rear.

She moved swiftly, leaving no chance for Phil to react.

In her hands was the only weapon Grandpa would allow in his house—the 1938 *Louisville Slugger*, the very one his father had given him. The same one he used when he taught me and Nicky to play ball on those long sun-filled days at his cottage, when he would be the father we never had, laughing and playing until we'd used up the last of his youthful vigour.

Phil never saw it coming.

One strike and he was out.

I ran for Dale, lifting him out of reach of the man we now knew to be a monster.

Phil groaned softly, stirring on the floor.

"Damn," Mom said.

"I can tie him up," I said.

"To hell with that."

She raised the bat once more, with steady surety, pausing for only an instant before bringing down the fatal blow.

Spent, she fell onto the couch. I think she was in shock. Her robe hung loosely, and she shivered. Her face was deadly white.

"Are you all right?" I asked.

Nicky brought a blanket from our room and covered her. I lifted her feet onto the couch.

"I'll be OK," she said. "Just give me a moment."

"We have to get him out of here," Nicky said, nodding at the bleeding mass that had been Phil.

I tried to take control of the situation, assuming my best television persona.

"I'll check his pulse," I said.

"Don't bother," Mom said, sitting up. "He's finished."

I thought she was probably right. His eyes were open, glazed over, staring blindly at the overhead fan.

"Give me the bat," Nicky said. "I'll clean it up."

"Good thinking," I said.

"I'll get dressed," Mom said.

"Me too. We can take him down to the dock."

"We have to take him further than that," she said. "We can use Grandpa's boat."

"I'll get the plastic tarp from the shed." My grandfather kept a couple of tarps, the kind you can tie to four trees to make an awning. We liked to sit under them when it rained, listening to the drops above our heads, all the while cheating nature by remaining outdoors and dry.

"There are rubber boots in the basement. Bring a pair for both of us."

"OK."

She headed for the master bedroom to get changed.

On my way to the stairs, I peeked into the bathroom. Nicky was doing a good job of cleaning the bat.

"I'm going to help Mom get rid of him," I said.

Nicky nodded.

"We'll leave Fanny with you and the boys. Can you clean the floor while we're gone?"

He nodded again.

"We can't leave any blood stains on the wood."

He knew what I meant. We both watched a lot of television.

"I'll move the furniture and make sure I get it all."

"Good. You'd better throw Mom's nightgown and robe into the washer. Dale and Fanny might need cleaning up, too. We'll try not to be too long."

"There's a deep spot over near where Mr. Branson likes to fish," Nicky said. "No one swims out that way."

"I know the spot."

"And John," he said, still scouring the bat, "make sure he stays down."

"I'll make sure."

In Grandpa's shed I found the wheelbarrow, some yellow nylon rope, a good, strong tarp and a cement block that had been broken in half.

I carried the tarp into the house. Nicky helped me roll Phil onto it. The floor under his head was still warm and slick. Then Nicky and Mom took one end of the tarp and I took the other, and together we carried him out to the yard.

We got both parts of the broken cement block into the tarp with Phil, then sealed it firmly with the heavy duty yellow rope before tipping the wheel barrow and rolling what was left of Phil into it. In the dark, we couldn't be sure we hadn't allowed any blood to escape, but we had no immediate neighbours. In the morning I'd come out and water the area, making sure to clean the wheel barrow.

"Boys, you mind Nicky while we're gone," Mom said to the twins. "Don't go into your room till you're clean."

They nodded.

I pushed the wheel barrow down to the dock. Phil was heavy, especially with the added weight of the cement block.

"That was good thinking," Mom said.

"Thanks."

She helped me get him into Grandpa's boat.

"I'll row," she said.

I was already bigger than she was, but I could tell her nerves were shot, so I didn't argue. Rowing gave her something to do.

We didn't talk much, at least not that I recall. When we were about half way to Branson's fishing spot, she paused in her rowing and looked up at the sky.

"Nearly a full moon," she said, taking care not to raise her voice. Sound carries easily on the water.

I looked to where she was pointing.

"I think it's supposed to be tomorrow night," I said.

"Johnny, tell me the truth. Was Phil molesting Dale?"

I looked away, studying the black water.

"I think so," I said.

"Me, too."

We found the spot, or near enough to it, and taking care not to tip the boat, we managed to roll him up and over the ledge.

He made a loud splash. It was over in a second. There aren't many people up that way, and even if anyone was awake, a splashing sound isn't unusual when you live near a lake.

"Well, that's that," Mom said.

"He'll stay down," I said.

"Would you mind rowing back? I'm kind of tired."

She traded spots with me and closed her eyes, turning her pale face up to the moonlight. I'd always thought of her as beautiful, and she was only thirty-one, but in that moment I could see the onset of age—the roots of tiredness spreading in tiny lines around her eyes.

Her blonde hair shone a ghostly silver, and I imagined: *This is how she'll look as an old woman. This is how she'll be in those last years before she dies.*

The thought made me sad.

I got us back as quickly as I could. Nicky was a tough bugger, but I knew the twins would be inconsolable, needing their mother.

I don't remember the rest of the weekend really. Mom called Grandpa on Saturday morning, spilling the whole story. He reminded her to go over everything with bleach, and he talked to me and the boys, telling us to stay calm.

"Don't panic," he said. "Cool heads will always prevail. Make sure you get rid of his belongings."

We stayed till Sunday night. Mom didn't want to raise suspicion by heading home early. We didn't do much—stayed in the cottage, close to Mom.

The drive back was long and quiet. We didn't make any stops.

We were all different somehow after that night. We went about our business in the usual way, keeping our routines. But a secret like that wears you down. We looked at each other with more knowing eyes.

Grandpa died a few years later. I don't know how I would've endured my teens without him—what kind of man I'd have become without his steady influence.

Nicky was, if possible, even more sullen in the years that followed, although he was a big help to Mom and me with the twins. He didn't like to leave them on their own—ever vigilant, I suppose—so he stayed close to home in the evenings, especially after I started dating.

Mom reported that a new salesperson from the drug manufacturing company had started calling on the pharmacy where she worked. A chatty young woman by the name of Selina. She and Mom became friends.

According to Selina, the previous salesperson, Phil, had up and disappeared, leaving the company without notice.

When police came around to speak to his co-workers, it was revealed Phil had a questionable history. He'd been accused on two separate occasions of impropriety towards children. In both cases, the victims and their single mothers had recanted. Charges were dropped.

Most likely, he'd been able to silence his previous victims with threats.

Phil met the wrong single mother the day he hooked up with Bessie Fender.

And now, more than twenty years later, I look out over the gathered congregation. Nicky isn't there. He joined the forces after high school and, like my father, never came back.

Dale and David remained bachelors. They have a house not far from Mom's. Today they're sitting in the front pew, together as always, near my wife, Samantha, and our daughter Bessie.

"My mother," I began, "believed in the irrepressible power of love."

My eyes sting. I'm not sure I can finish the eulogy.

But I know I must, and so I reach down deep inside myself for the courage to say goodbye…

…to the strongest, most loving person I will ever know.

About Donna Carrick

An Air Force Brat, Donna grew up in locations all over Canada. Her primary influences came from small town Saskatchewan, Northern Ontario, the mining towns of Cape Breton, Northern Quebec and her birth province of New Brunswick.

Donna is the author of: *The First Excellence*, *Gold And Fishes* and *The Noon God*.

Her anthologies, *Sept-Iles and other places* and *Knowing Penelope*, are available for Kindle. She also compiled and edited *EFD1: Starship Goodwords* (Carrick Publishing), a cross-genre collection of stories and poems.

An executive member of Crime Writers of Canada, Donna volunteers her time as a mentor to aspiring CWC authors. She remains active in the Canadian writing scene, supporting Sisters in Crime, Word on the Street, Bloody Words and a variety of other venues for the literary arts.

Connect with Donna at:
http://www.donnacarrick.com/
http://www.carrickpublishing.com/
FaceBook: Donna Carrick
Twitter: @Donna_Carrick
www.mesdamesofmayhem.com

The Canadian Caper

by Rosemary Aubert

At it again!

Mrs. DiRosa manoeuvred her walker so that it was flush against the sill of the hallway window on the sixth floor of The Towers—called Wobble Towers by her smarty-pants grandchildren. It was the only way she could free both hands in order to adjust her binoculars. *Damn cheap things. If they made them here, instead of some foreign country, they'd work better.*

She fiddled with them until she could see the Canadian flag clear as a bell on the other side of the river. That was one of the things her daughter said was so great about The Towers. That you could get such a good view of the bridge from Niagara Falls, New York to Niagara Falls, Canada.

"Could be the only place in the world where you can look out a window and see another country," her helpful son-in-law had suggested when they'd signed her in.

Big deal!

She trained the binoculars on a vehicle stopped at the Canadian toll booth and gave the focus knob one more little shove. *Good thing I don't have arthritis!* She tracked the long truck full of logs as it slowly made its way through the narrow entrance and onto the bridge.

"You still looking at them trucks?"

At the squeaky-voiced question coming from behind, Mrs. DiRosa jumped a mile. She let the binoculars fall back around her neck by their cord and grabbed her walker, turning to face the only person she could stand in The Towers, her friend Meenie—or Teenie Meenie as Mrs. DiRosa's grandchildren called their grandmother's seventy-five-pound friend. Her real name was Minette, and a long time ago she'd left her home in Canada to live with her children before she, too, had been sent to The Towers. She still spoke with a French Canadian accent.

"What do you have to sneak up on me like that for?" Mrs. DiRosa said irritably. "Scared the dickens out of me and messed up my focus, too."

"You still watchin' them truckloads of frogs?"

"Logs, you silly old thing. Not frogs, logs."

"So why you watchin' them now?" Meenie asked.

"Look," Mrs. DiRosa said, forgetting her disgruntlement and eager to share her remarkable discovery. "See that truck coming through now?"

She handed the binoculars to Meenie who, being ten years younger, was more agile in every way and had no need of a walker to help her get close to the window. She held the binoculars to her eyes.

"Yeah, I see it," she said, "It just got to the American side. One of them nice-looking young men in the uniform is talking to the driver. So what?"

"Get a load of the very top log. See anything funny about it?"

Meenie was quiet for a few seconds. Studying. "I see a mark on the top log," she finally said. "A funny mark. Maybe like a hax hit it wrong."

"Axe," Mrs. DiRosa said. She had been correcting Meenie's English now for eighteen and a half years without any noticeable effect. "Yes, that's it."

"What's funny about a hax mark on a big log?"

"Nothing," Mrs. DiRosa said. "Except that I've seen that mark on that log six times since I started counting."

"What?"

"Meenie, that truck comes through here once every two weeks. And every single time, the same log is on top."

Meenie leaned closer to the window. "Comes down from Canada with the same log on top? I don't get it."

Mrs. DiRosa took the binoculars from her friend's hand. She trained them on the handsome young American customs official. She watched as he took a bunch of papers from the driver of the truck, glanced at them, nodded and waved the man on.

"They don't keep them long enough with nine-eleven and all," Mrs. DiRosa said. "No wonder there's so many smugglers."

Meenie laughed. "You read too many of them books. You got too much of imagination. There aren't smugglers now. That's stuff out of stories."

"No, it isn't," Mrs. DiRosa said, suddenly remembering bits and pieces of a conversation. "Somebody was talking about smuggling just last week."

Damn memory. Isn't worth a thing. Should have eaten more carrots or something.

Meenie thought about it for just a minute. "I know," she said. "It was at the Trans-border Social last Tuesday. You know, when those old ladies come over from Canada for lunch at The Towers."

"Yes, Meenie. You're right. That's it! They were talking about smuggling people out of foreign countries through Canada into the United States!"

"You don't think that truck of logs has people hid in it?"

Mrs. DiRosa took another look out the window. The log truck was just pulling onto the Parkway, headed for points south. "The logs could be hollow or something like that. I wouldn't be surprised. Foreigners are tricky. And getting into America is the thing they want most."

"But it's a big crime!" Meenie protested.

"Sure is," Mrs. DiRosa said. She caught one last glimpse of the truck as it disappeared down the highway. "A whole load of criminals headed right into the heart of America."

It wasn't until the next day that Mrs. DiRosa finally figured out what they had to do. "Meenie, you've got to talk to that nice young customs man."

Meenie laughed. "What I going to tell him—that my friend think people are coming in empty logs to America?"

"Don't be a smarty-pants. I'd do it myself only I can't walk. You can."

"But I can't talk that good. He won't listen. He'll just think I'm some old crazy person like Mr. Winters."

Mr. Winters no longer lived at The Towers because he'd wandered onto the bridge in his underwear on a February morning, swearing he was Canadian and wanted to die at home.

Meenie's got a point.

"OK," Mrs. DiRosa said, "I've got it. I'll write everything in a letter. How I've been watching the bridge for weeks now and have seen the same truck with the same logs go over time after time. I'll put in the letter about how I can see that top log from above, which is how I can tell it's the same log, when the customs men can't. Then they won't feel insulted or anything."

"Don't want to insult them, no," Meenie agreed.

"Then you'll do it?"

"To keep criminals out of America? OK."

It didn't take long to write the letter. Meenie was right about Mrs. DiRosa reading a lot of books. One thing it did for you was make it easy to write. She signed the letter, "An American Citizen." That sounded good.

Even though it would take Meenie a while to go all the way downstairs, then to the back door, then across the parking lot, then across the street, then onto the bridge and into the customs booth, Mrs. DiRosa got right up against the window the minute Meenie left her apartment.

It seemed to take forever before she finally caught sight of her. Luckily it wasn't a busy day on the bridge. Even without the binoculars, Mrs. DiRosa could see the customs man take the envelope from Meenie. She watched him tear it open and read the letter. Then she saw him step into the booth and pick up the telephone. She lifted the binoculars. Now she could see that the man was smiling and nodding. Was he talking to his boss? Were they going to check things out?

She waited for what seemed like a long time. Finally the man put down the phone. He stepped out of the booth. He had something in his hand, which he gave to Meenie. He was talking to her. Mrs. DiRosa couldn't see Meenie's face too clearly. But she did see that Meenie's shoulders were more slumped than usual. It didn't seem like a good sign. It wasn't a good sign either when the handsome young customs man patted Meenie on the head just like she was a dog.

"All he did was give me this," Meenie said, holding up a small, bright American flag.

"What did he *say*?" Mrs. DiRosa demanded. They'd already been through this several times, but she wanted to make sure.

"I *told* you," Meenie said, twirling the flag in her fingers until Mrs. DiRosa reached out and made her stop. "He say old ladies don't always see too good and not to worry because he's protecting America for us."

Mrs. DiRosa thought about it for one minute longer. Then she made up her mind. "That log truck has something wrong about it and I'm not going to give up until we find out what it is."

"How come you always say 'we'?" Meenie asked, beginning to twirl the flag again.

"There's only one thing *we* can do now," Mrs. DiRosa announced.

"Oh, no. What?"

"*We* have to go to Canada."

"But you can't even walk!"

"*We* will find a way."

"Stop saying we," Meenie said again, but of course, Mrs. DiRosa wasn't listening. She was thinking again.

The first thing they had to do was borrow a wheelchair from the office. It wasn't easy because for several years now, Mrs. DiRosa had told the The Towers' social worker that the only place she was going to be wheeled was to her grave.

"Where you be goin' then, sweetie?" the social worker asked. She was a nice young girl with a master's degree in social work from some university in Georgia.

Too bad they don't teach English in college any more. "To the library," Mrs. DiRosa lied, and Meenie, who was standing behind her, nodded.

"Well, you all be careful now, you hear?"

"Of course," both the old women said sweetly and simultaneously.

"Good, we fooled her," Mrs. DiRosa told Meenie as she got herself down into the chair and arranged a blanket around her legs. "Now we've got to get going. The plan's simple. We just wheel right on out the back door, over the parking lot, across the street—be sure to watch both ways—and onto the bridge. On the American side we've just got to pay the toll—no questions asked. Once we get over to Canada, I'll tell them you don't speak any English. That way I can do all the talking."

"What if they find out we're missing from The Towers?" Meenie wasn't nearly as sure of the plan as Mrs. DiRosa.

"No problem. Today's Tuesday—Trans-border Social day. It's Canada's turn. I signed us both up. That bus driver's so lazy, he never checks how many there are. And if the Canadians have any questions, we just say we missed the Trans-border Social Club bus."

Meenie shook her head. "I don't think…"

"You don't have to think," Mrs. DiRosa said. "You just have to push."

It was cold going across the bridge even though it was the middle of June. The wind off the river smelled a certain way that Mrs. DiRosa remembered from long ago. It had been almost twenty years since she'd gone across the bridge in any way except by her daughter and son-in-law's car. She remembered Mr. DiRosa and all the times they went to Canada together in the old days, bringing back good Canadian tea, jam, cheese and toffee that killed your teeth and—for the Fourth of July—nice Canadian firecrackers that you had to hide under your blouse to get across. The memory of it made tears come to her eyes and the tears gave her a good idea.

"Don't say a thing, Meenie," Mrs. DiRosa reminded her friend as they came within a few yards of the Canadian customs booth. They could see the outline of a person behind the glass of the booth, but when the person stepped out with a little smile on her face, Mrs. DiRosa was surprised. She'd expected the Canadian customs officer to be a handsome young man just like the American one. Only it was a young woman instead. A smart-looking young woman.

"Well now, ladies, what can I do for you?" the girl said. She looked friendly, but suspicious, too. Mrs. DiRosa was glad about the new angle to her plan.

She sniffled and squeezed her eyes shut, and made a few of the tears that were still in her eyes run down her cheeks. "I have come home to die," she said.

She could feel the back of the wheelchair wiggle a little bit, but Meenie kept her mouth shut.

The young woman looked shocked. "Come in here, ladies," she said, her voice a little shaky, "just wait for a moment, please."

She opened the door to the customs office. Meenie wheeled Mrs. DiRosa in. The customs officer disappeared down a narrow hall.

The minute she was out of sight, Meenie came around the front of the wheelchair. She was good and mad. "What's the matter with you?" she demanded of Mrs. DiRosa. "Why you tell them such a crazy thing? You want to be like Mr. Winters? How that fix the smugglers?"

"Calm down," Mrs. DiRosa said. "Remember how they got all those officials to come to the bridge when old Winters went crazy? They'll call the same ones now. The minute the bigwigs get here, we'll spill the beans."

They heard footsteps coming down the hall, the light steps of the female officer and then heavier steps.

"Here they come."

It was in all the papers: the *Niagara Gazette*, the *Buffalo Evening News*, even the papers up in Toronto and the *Pennysaver*. Mrs. DiRosa cut out the articles and taped them up on her wall. They showed her and Meenie talking to a reporter, and they said how they'd tipped off the bridge guards and broken up a ring of people smugglers.

Mrs. DiRosa's daughter was hopping mad at first. "I signed you up at The Towers so you would be safe, and look what you do—running off after smugglers."

"I didn't run after them, I just turned them in," Mrs. DiRosa said.

"Well, I'm taking those binoculars away right now. I don't want you to put yourself at risk like this ever again."

Mrs. DiRosa thought fast. "I'll give them in to the penny sale," she said. "Then somebody else can benefit by them."

Her daughter was about to answer that when the phone rang. It was a TV reporter from New York. She forgot about the binoculars when she found out Mrs. DiRosa was going to be on the news right across the country.

"You're hot now, Grandma," her grandchildren said when they heard that.

Smarty-pants.

Mrs. DiRosa manoeuvred her walker so that it was flush against the windowsill. She lifted the binoculars to her eyes.

"What you lookin' at now? More trucks?"

"'Course not," she said to Meenie. "I'm just checking to make sure these are all right before I give them in for the penny sale. You know how mad that social worker gets when people donate things that don't work."

Mrs. DiRosa leaned against the walker and freed her other hand to fiddle with the focus. She could see the Canadian flag clear as a bell across the river.

Good thing they teach people to respect their elders in Canada.

That's what she was thinking when she saw it again. Just as she had seen it twice before: a van driven by a man pulled into one of the parking lots a little ways down the river from the entrance to the bridge. The man seemed to disappear into the back of the van. Then after a little while, the front door of the van opened and a woman walked out. No sign of the man anymore. Like he had up and disappeared altogether. The woman walked toward the bridge, paid the toll and began to walk over the bridge right toward America.

"Lots of crooks in this world, Meenie," Mrs. DiRosa said.

"We gonna need that wheelchair again?" Meenie asked.

Could be, Meenie, could be....

About Rosemary Aubert

Rosemary Aubert is the author of sixteen books, among them the acclaimed *Ellis Portal mystery series* and her latest romantic thriller *Terminal Grill*. Rosemary is a two-time winner of the Arthur Ellis Award for crime fiction, winning in both the novel and short-story categories.

She's a popular teacher and speaker. Rosemary is a member of the Crime Writers of Canada and the Mystery Writers of America. She conducts a much-in-demand writers' retreat at Loyalist College in Belleville, Ontario each summer, as well as mentoring writing students at the School of Continuing Studies at the University of Toronto.

Rosemary is an active member of the Arts and Letters Club of Toronto where she promotes Canadian writing and encourages other writers like herself.

Connect with Rosemary at:
Website: www.rosemaryaubert.com
Quattro Books
Amazon.ca
Chapters-Indigo
www.mesdamesofmayhem.com

July is Hell

by Melodie Campbell

I came back to the squad car with two coffees, both black.

Bill was fanning himself with yesterday's newspaper. "It's frigging middle of the night, for crissake. How can it still be so hot?"

I shrugged. "July is hell. Always will be." I passed him the cup of java.

"This job is hell," Bill muttered, leaning back in the seat. His thick body showed the wear and tear of thirty years on the job. He removed the lid carefully and threw it on the dash. Then he sighed. "I've got bad news for you."

I was alert now. Looking keen.

His grey eyebrows creased into a frown. "You know that perp who raped those young girls back in March?"

I nodded. Of course I knew. We had worked that case around the clock.

Bill looked at me, then quickly away. "They got him off on a technicality."

I cursed. We'd tracked him for weeks. We knew he was guilty, even if he had worn a balaclava. It was all in the way he reacted when we arrested him. You just know. That smile…

"I know," Bill mumbled. "Damned lawyers. Time for me to get out of this hellhole. Do something positive with the rest of my life."

"So you're really going to retire, then?"

He nodded. "This case made up my mind. I'm finished with it." He looked over at me. "You have your own decisions to make. You're young. You sure you want to stay in this game?"

I made a point of looking serious. "It's what I do, Bill. What I've always wanted to do."

He shook his head. Then he took another sip. "Just be careful you don't get completely disillusioned like I am. It's not healthy. Letting scum like that go free on a technicality." He snorted in disgust.

"He'll go to hell when he's dead," I said evenly.

"You really believe that stuff?" Bill's voice was soft. "Well, you just go on believing it, Chris. Maybe it will keep you sane."

I doubt it, I thought to myself. I doubted it again when I took a knife to the perp's throat the next night.

It took me only a few hours to track him down. That's the advantage of being a cop and a woman. You know how to find people, you know how to kill, and you know how to cover your tracks.

He was going to hell all right, but I swear it was just as hot here.

Melodie Campbell

Triskaidekaphobia

by Jane Petersen Burfield

"Four No Trump."

"Are you sure, Annie?" asked her partner nervously. June was still floundering through the higher demands of bridge. She had been recruited as a temporary replacement at Friday Bridge while Jennie was away.

"Four No," Annie said again. "And you know what to do, June."

At the table, on June's left, Margie grinned at her partner, Edna. With few points between them, they knew the other team could make almost any bridge contract if they concentrated on their play. Maybe they could be distracted by talk.

"Have you heard the latest about Jennie, June? You know, Jennie who usually plays with us. The one who had the miserable husband. And the mother-in-law from hell."

Edna winked at Margie, but June and Annie were too involved in counting the tricks in their hands to notice. And so, after a final contract of six no trump was declared, Margie began her story while they played.

"The last time Jennie wore black was at her husband's funeral, and then she only wore black because it was expected of a new widow. In her heart, she told me, she was wearing a rainbow of ice cream shades, colours that reflected her stepping into a garden of new hope, new feeling, new thought. Jennie said she felt free for the first time in more than twenty years.

"Mort, or Morley to his mother, met Jennie at York, when it was a new university in the north end of Toronto. It was a second choice university for most students, but a school where flexible degree choices also attracted adventuresome undergrads and professors.

"They met in a course only masochists would take, 'Milton, Shakespeare and Blake as Political Vessels of Their Times'. Mort liked the reference to vessels: it made him think of beer. Jennie took this behemoth of a course as an academic challenge. They were both part of the few who passed in spite of the best efforts of their prof, who was trying to establish his academic reputation by failing as many students as possible.

"Jennie wore a blue dress and shoes to the first seminar. With her bright red hair, she was a stand-out. Mort, used to the conservative shades of his home, thought Jennie was exotic and fun, and decided he wanted to get to know her. Jennie was finally out of the grey school uniform she had worn for more than ten years—and she loved colour.

"Mort stalked her, always managing to be outside the lecture hall door when she was leaving class. Oblivious to his attention, Jennie was polite. It was a very long courtship before he proposed.

"Jennie wanted a wedding not full of poufy dresses and even grander pretensions, but one that led to a solid married life. Mort wanted a wedding and reception with enough flair to be memorable to his parents and their friends. When they married in Jennie's United Church, Jennie left out the 'obey' part of 'Love, honour and'. Shirley, Mort's mother, was not pleased. And when Mort said his vows, he winked when he promised love and fidelity. At the time, Jennie just thought it was cute.

"Thus they began their slow journey into married mediocrity. They had the required two children, a girl and a boy, the so-called 'millionaire's family'. Mort bought life and mortgage insurance so his family would be secure. Their house, a four bed centre hall decorated in discreet beige, was approved for both its layout and location. Jennie had wanted to settle in the Beach area of Toronto, but that location was judged as too bohemian, and too far from Mort's new job in a consulting business. So a small house in Lawrence Park it was.

"Jennie wanted to use her fine arts degree when she worked. She enjoyed exploring new art ideas and teaching children, and she'd developed a good eye for colour and composition in her undergrad courses. Colour made her feel happy. Mort and his mom thought she should stay at home, initially to decorate the house and make connections with other young marrieds at the country club, and then to take care of the kids. A few years later when Jennie pointed out that the kids were now old enough to be at school all day, Mort told her he expected her to keep a clean house, have a good meal on the table, and be prepared to entertain clients and friends on short notice. So Jennie sank further into a dark space quite foreign to her adventuresome self. She felt bound, like Gulliver, in a soulless place.

"Jennie rarely noticed anymore when Mort flirted with the young waitresses at the club. She thought that, like much else about Mort, it was all bluster. She knew he was becoming one of those men she had disliked so much, one who flirted constantly and had hands that strayed where they shouldn't. She didn't understand why he was changing. They had a lovely home, two great kids, and he had a good job. But Mort did not seem satisfied with his life.

"Jennie decided to try to add some colour to her own life by painting in her basement 'studio' at the far end of the laundry room. But it's hard to be creative under neon tube lights. Mort objected to the smell of turpentine. Jennie took up water colours.

"And then one day at Sally's school, she was asked to help plan a reception for visiting students from Japan. The principal wanted to showcase Toronto and Canada in a mural to be designed and painted by the students. Jennie got out her pencil and pad, and set off to meet the chosen two artists from each classroom, kids who needed a boost in self-esteem. With some lively discussion, they created a drawing with maple leaves, the Maple Leaf hockey team and the CN Tower at its core.

"The feat of guiding the kids in choosing images to represent life in the city was fulfilling. Jennie was late getting home that evening, late in preparing the meal and creating the candlelit ambiance Mort wanted when he hosted dinner for business clients. He was not pleased. He drank a little too much and flirted with the client's girlfriend. The contract was never signed.

"Jennie returned to the school the next day, refreshed and eager to gather and sort more ideas for the border of the mural. The students sent to participate became more enthusiastic, and her small project became mainstream at the school. And as Jennie worked with these slightly marginalized kids on their images, she felt alive. Life was so much more pleasant when Mort wasn't imposing his needs all the time.

"In one small matter of her home life, Jennie had won an argument. Mort insisted he wanted no animals in the house as they were dirty, triggered allergies, and took too much time and money to care for. Jennie tried to talk it over, suggesting the kids would benefit from the responsibility and from the love. Mort was adamant. But when he came back from a business trip a few weeks later, a small black kitten greeted him with a hiss and a flurry of attacking claws. Mort threatened to drown it, but Jennie and the kids hid it until Mort got so involved in his current deal, he forgot about the new pet. So Trisky became a small wedge of affection and fun for Jennie and the kids, and a constant annoyance for Mort, who even hated the cat's name. He thought the name too cute.

"Trisky was more than just an annoyance to Mort. He was a black cat, one of the more unlucky icons to a superstitious man. Mort rarely mentioned his superstitions to outsiders, but his family knew about his illogical dislike of black animals, broken mirrors and anything to do with the number thirteen.

"Mort's business became more successful. He decided they needed a bigger home with an extra bedroom for his mother. House hunting was a disaster. Something was always wrong with the layout, or the landscaping, or the condition of the shutters. In reality, Jennie realized, the houses broke his unwritten rules of superstition. When they viewed the last house, Jennie caught Mort counting the stairs. When he announced 'twelve' for the number of steps down the main staircase, Jennie felt relief. The house was perfect. She never pointed out to Mort that the step up into their master suite off the mid-landing made thirteen stairs. He never would have bought the house, and she liked it.

"Mort may have inherited his superstitions from his mother, who was as ridiculously afraid of black cats as she was attached to knocking on wood and carrying a rabbit's foot. When Trisky grabbed her rabbit foot key ring, and began carrying it around the house, Shirley refused to go out as she knew bad luck would stalk her. It took two days to get her out of her bedroom. Jennie viewed that time as a mini-vacation.

"The kids loved the cat's antics, and they needed some fun at home. Sally, the elder, was beginning her final high school year, a year full of impossible demands from her teachers and from her guidance counsellor. Home life was not pleasant. She spent as much time as possible at her friend's house to avoid her father's and grandmother's bickering. Shirley and Mort battled about Jennie's inadequacies, about the deficiencies in their lifestyle, and about the cat.

"Mike, in grade nine, was insecure in his new high school life, and was, Jennie suspected, being bullied. He retreated into social media and online battle games to vent his frustration. Neither of them needed Mort to berate them for a lack of accomplishment, or a lack of social graces or appearance. Jennie could do little to stop Mort, as he bullied her the same way, but she would try to make her kids feel better. And she did feel better, until Mike asked her why she stayed with Mort. Fear, she thought. Fear about finances, but she didn't answer him.

"As the atmosphere in the house thickened with dislike and growing frustration, Jennie decided she had to do something. Something, but what?

"The next week, Mort announced he was moving his office to Huntsville. He said he had wasted enough time in the city, and needed the change and new challenge up north. He said he could do his work online. Jennie thought Mort might be using the move as an excuse to get rid of a bothersome assistant who had become a little too close. Mort had not even asked her what she thought, Jennie noted, although he had obviously discussed it with his dear Mama.

"Jennie liked going to Muskoka in the summer for several weeks, but to live there year round would be difficult, especially if she went back to university. The commute up and down would be horrendous in winter. And with the kids settled into schools in Toronto, moving up north midway through the year would be disruptive.

"'Could we delay the move, Mort?' Jennie asked. 'I'd like a chance to get our lives organized down here. The kids need to finish school.'

"Mort sat back, sipping his drink. 'Sally's off to university in the fall, and Mike can go to the high school up there. We need a change. We can join the Muskoka Club, which is much less expensive than the Granite. And Mother really wants to go back there. That's where she grew up, you remember.'

"Jennie paused, thinking carefully how to phrase her request. 'I would like to finish my art project at the school, and to get the house ready for sale. I also want to complete my Masters before we leave the city. And it would only take a year or so. What's the hurry?'

"Mort barely looked in her direction as he flipped the channels on the television remote. 'Mother wants to go now, and I'm fed up with my partners here. They want to buy me out, but not for as much as I'd like, so we can't afford to live here. Besides, think of the golf and the fishing.'

"I can hardly wait, Jennie thought. She wondered what he had done to upset his partners enough to boot him out. Was the assistant threatening blackmail about their affair? Jennie didn't really care if Mort fooled around. She had long ago given up hope for a loving relationship. But she was furious that his lack of control was probably the main reason she'd be uprooted from her own friendships and connections. Jennie loathed club life, golf and fishing in more or less that order. She needed to think.

"The Ladies League Friday Bridge gave her relief. While playing cards each week, she could discuss her life. The ladies were discreet as they all knew each other's secrets. Jennie especially enjoyed dressing up and conversing in an old world environment.

"One Friday, after a particularly draining week at home, she decided to go shopping after bridge with her friends. When a fetching pair of red Christian Louboutin shoes, ones with impossibly long, pointed toes, appeared on sale, Jennie bought them in spite of their ridiculous price as a small rebellion against Mort's sudden economy. Mort liked her to dress conservatively. She knew he would hate the red shoes, but she no longer cared.

"Jennie wore her red shoes for the client dinner the next week. Mort groused, but after seeing the client's wife chatting with Jennie about her shoes, he held fire. But Mort was not happy, for he had been trumped. Jennie kept the shoes.

"Early in May during a week when Mort was particularly cranky, Trisky played on the stairs and sang to her catnip mouse the way a feral cat sings to its prey before killing it. Mort sat up in bed, woke Jennie and told her to silence 'that animal' or he would, once and for all. Jennie called to the little furball. Trisky shot through their bedroom door, belled catnip mouse in her mouth, and leaped up onto their bed. Mort kicked out, but Trisky was too quick. She jumped to Jennie's side of the bed where she settled contentedly. Trisky had developed the trick of always getting on Mort's nerves and under his feet, but dancing out of reach quickly. She had grown into a beautiful, young cat with long black fur and a plume of a tail. Mort always looked at her suspiciously. Black cats were one of his greatest fears.

"Mort got up for one of his now frequent trips to the bathroom, relying on his 'fabled' night vision, and not putting on the light. When he came out of the bathroom and headed back to bed, Trisky decided to dash past, twisting around Mort's feet. In quiet fury, Mort kicked out and sent Trisky flying. He swore he was taking the cat to be put down the next morning.

"Jennie had put up with Mort's demands for years. But she wasn't ready to be uprooted from her friends and leave her family. And she was not going to let her little furball be put down for being an inconvenience. She had to act."

"What about Jennie's family?" asked June as she put down her cards.

"We never heard much about Jennie's family. I know her dad died when she was quite young. Her mother was an herbalist and aromatherapist, a bit strange. Jennie's sister helped her mother in the candle and speciality shop they owned. Jennie wanted to do something different, and ended up with the ineffable Mort. I think she should have stuck with herbs and candles."

The ladies gathered up the cards after June and Annie went down two tricks. As Edna shuffled, Margie continued the story while she dealt.

"Next day, Jennie dressed for Friday Bridge, and put on her navy suit and pearls. And then she got out the red Louboutin shoes, the ones Mort hated, and added a red scarf. Downstairs, Mort and Shirley told her she looked ridiculous, but Jennie ignored them. She knew how she felt.

And she was so fed up with their criticism that she wanted to do just the opposite.

"As she went upstairs to get her handbag, Trisky followed, full of frolic. Mort came up the stairs, counting as he always did. One, two, three, up to twelve. At the top of the stairs, he went to step up into the bedroom, the thirteenth step, when Trisky sprang out at him, flicking his trousers with her claws. Jennie was standing beside the doorway. As Mort tried to turn, he tripped over her extended foot, fell backwards off the bedroom step, and catapulted down the stairs into his mother who was just coming up.

"The paramedics said he broke his neck at the bottom, and his mother hit her head against the wall. There was nothing they could do for either of them.

"The police questioned Jennie. They had been told by Mort's aunt that the marriage was not happy. But Jennie's version of what happened was consistent with the evidence, and so the deaths were deemed accidental.

"Jennie told me that she always liked a two for one deal. And the scuff mark on her special red shoes could be covered with polish.

"She's been much happier the last few months. The insurance paid off Mort's debts and the mortgage, his partners were forced to buy out his portion of the business, and there is enough left to get the kids through college and give her a modest income. Perhaps even enough money for a new catnip mouse for Trisky, and a new pair of Louboutins for Jennie."

"The cat has a peculiar name, Margie", June said. "Is Trisky a combination of frisky and tricky?"

"Oh no," Margie said. "It's short for Triskaidekaphobia. The fear of thirteen. Mort had a lot of superstitions, but he always said thirteen would do him in."

About Jane Petersen Burfield

Killing someone softly with words is greatly appealing to a North Toronto matron like Jane. After raising three wonderful daughters in a fourth generation family home, she is ready for more adventure. Finding a way to use fashion, vegetables and small animals in her stories to bring about justice, albeit rough justice, is her challenge.

To her utter amazement, Jane won the Bony Pete Short Story Award in 2001 for *"Slow Death and Taxes"*, the first short story she wrote. After several more years of success with the Bloody Words story contest, she decided writing was a misery-making but delightful challenge. She has had short stories published in *Blood on the Holly* and *Bloody Words, the Anthology*.

Jane is honoured to be a member of Mesdames of Mayhem, and looks forward to the creative buzz that comes from an association of women writers. She hopes you enjoy her story about a woman creating her own justice.

Connect with Jane at:
FaceBook: Jane Burfield
www.mesdamesofmayhem.com

Amdur's Cat

by M. H. Callway

On a snowy December night Benjamin Amdur saw a lion. It was gamboling about like a kitten swatting at the fat, wet snowflakes that tumbled through the dark. Right in the centre of Riverdale Park by the children's wading pool.

Under the lamps of the park's snowy pathway, the lion's tawny fur glowed like the back of an old velvet sofa. For a brief moment—that gap between the surreal world and biting reality—he watched Rousseau's painted lion come to life.

Then he remembered the sleeping gypsy—the minstrel who was about to be eaten.

He grasped the icy black iron fence beside him. The house it surrounded lay dark. At two in the morning, its inhabitants, like most normal people, were in bed. By the time he woke them up screaming for help, the lion would have torn out his throat.

With infinite caution, his eyes on the animal, he edged back into the shadows of Winchester Street, the road he'd weaved down moments before. Behind him, three blocks away, lay Parliament Street with its strip bars, eateries and mini-marts. Surely to God one of those places had to be open!

The lion leapt in the air. It snapped at the snowflakes as they fell. He heard the crunch of its jaws, saw the flash of its teeth. Its tail lashed back and forth.

Then it paused, raised its huge head and sniffed the air. Its nostrils twitched.

It saw me!

Amdur turned and ran like a mad man.

Adrenalin buoyed him up for the first few feet, but deserted him almost immediately. He was forty-eight and twenty pounds overweight. His regular habit of walking to work did nothing to bolster his panic-stricken need to run. He tore down the slushy sidewalk, his mind fixed on the zebras of the veldt. Zebras that ran far more swiftly than he. Zebras brought down and eviscerated alive...

By the time he reached the yellow lights of Parliament Street his chest was heaving. He doubled over, gasping for oxygen. If the lion got him now, he was dinner. But he couldn't take another step.

He looked frantically up and down the street. Every storefront was dark.

No buses, no taxis, no cars.

Then he spotted an angel standing under a streetlight a few yards to the south. Well, not an angel exactly, but a young police officer, her uniform immaculate, the brim of her cap spotless, her leather boots and gun holster gleaming with polish.

He summoned his remaining strength and stumbled over to her. "Oh, thank God...an animal...danger..." He couldn't stop panting. "Very dangerous. Over by ...Riverdale Farm."

She raised a tidy eyebrow. "Are you quite all right, sir?"

"No...no, I'm not all right." With the dispassion of his medical training, he estimated his heart to be thumping at 180 beats per minute. His blood pressure didn't bear thinking about. "You…help…must get help."

"How much have you had to drink tonight, sir?"

"Drink?" he echoed.

"Quite a few, I'd say. Identification, please."

"What?" Finally he caught his breath. "Please, you don't understand. There's a bloody great animal running around loose. It'll rip someone apart. We have to stop it."

"Your ID. Now!" Her hand moved toward her baton.

Amdur dragged out his wallet and handed her his driver's license. Her laser stare burned through its laminate cover.

"Dr. Benjamin Amdur." She studied his face with more than an element of disbelief. "So you're a doctor."

"Yes, I'm with the Ministry of Health. I'm Assistant Deputy Minister in charge of OHIP."

That made no impression on her whatsoever. "OHIP?"

"Your, I mean, *our* free medicine in Ontario. Look here, we're wasting time."

"How many drinks have you had tonight, sir?"

"What the hell does it matter? I was at a Christmas party, for heaven's sake. At the National Club." That lofty name made even less impression on her. "I tell you I know what I saw. There's a lion on the loose."

"Lion! Why didn't you say so!"

"I did say so."

"Where? Where did you see it?"

"In Riverdale Park, by the children's wading pool…the farm."

She shoved his license in her tunic and tore down Winchester Street, leaving him standing there like an idiot.

He chased after her, but she set a blistering pace. He only managed to catch up with her at the edge of the park.

No sign of the lion.

Amdur squinted through the heavy curtain of falling snow. Where was the beast? Where was it? The grounds of the park stretched out before him, white and featureless under the thick drifts.

"I don't see any lion." The police officer scanned the area with her hard dark eyes. "Show me exactly where you saw him."

"Right over there!" Amdur pointed to the spot.

"OK, let's go. You first."

"I don't think that's wise."

"I'll be the judge of that." She straightened her cap. "Get going or I'll arrest you. For wasting police time."

"Fine, fine."

The pathway lay buried in snow. He trudged through the heavy wet drifts toward the dark shapes of Riverdale Farm, a miserable King Wenceslas with his testy page behind him.

By the time they arrived at the snowed-in wading pool, he was thoroughly chilled. "The lion was here." He scanned the ground for paw prints but saw nothing. "He was running around right here, I swear it. The snow must have covered his tracks."

"Right, sure. One side." She pushed past him, bending down to study the snow drift in front of them. Suddenly she stiffened. "Did you hear that?"

"No, nothing." The falling snow muffled all sound.

"Over there." She pointed to a tangled clump of bushes a few feet away, stood up and unbuttoned her gun holster. "Stay here." She headed for the bushes.

"Wait! For heaven's sake, call for back-up."

She vanished behind the twisted mass of branches. The lion must be behind it, lurking...

Amdur fumbled for his Blackberry. Why had he trusted that inexperienced young constable? She was going to get them both killed.

He tried to punch out 911, but the phone slithered from his frozen hands and plopped into the snow. He kneeled down and foraged desperately for it. By the time his numb fingers retrieved it, he was staring at the police officer's polished boots.

He stumbled to his feet. "You're back. You're all right."

"Score ten out of ten, Captain Obvious. You can put your phone away now."

"Where's the lion? Did you see him?"

"Oh, yeah, right. The lion. Sure, I saw him. Teeth like a raptor. I've got him right here."

He noticed belatedly that she was clutching a furry wet bag in her arms. The bag came to life with a piercing cry.

"Here, take him."

Before he had a chance to react, she heaved the soaking bundle at him. It thudded against his chest. Long, curved claws dug into his cashmere overcoat.

"That's a cat!"

"No kidding."

"I didn't see a cat. I saw a lion!"

"Right, sure you did. Time to go home. You first." She pointed the way out of the park.

"This isn't my cat. I don't own a cat." He tried in vain to detach the animal's claws. "Look, I can't just take him."

"Fine, doctor." The word 'doctor' rang with the respect she no doubt reserved for pimps and pederasts.

"Here's your choice. Either you take your cat home all nice and quiet or I throw you in the drunk tank. How about that? I bet that'd go down real well with your fancy-ass friends at the National Club."

"For God's sake!" He gripped the cat with his free hand and shoved his phone back into his coat pocket with the other. He felt exhausted—and admittedly too well-oiled—to argue any further.

She'd read his address from the front of his driver's license, so she knew exactly where he lived. He stumbled out of the park to Sumach Street, then north to the tall brick Victorian house that held his flat. Both she and the cat stuck with him up to the front door.

"Keys!" She held out a gloved hand.

Swearing, he clutched the cat with one chilled hand, dug out his keys with the other and handed them over.

Once safe inside his flat, he tried to detach the cat, but it let out a terrifying howl.

"Damn it, the cat will wake the other tenants. What do I do?"

She laughed and tossed his keys down on the hardwood floor next to his soaking feet. "Dry him off and feed him. Give him tuna. Cats like tuna."

"And what the hell do I do about his other end?"

"Tear up some newspaper. Throw it in a box. And don't forget, Dr. Amdur. I know where you live." She snapped the edge of his driver's license and flipped it down onto the floor next to his keys.

With that, she slammed his front door shut and left.

And he'd taken her for an angel! She was a demon, a witch—and this wretched lump of wetness attached to his chest was her familiar.

He lurched down the hall to the bathroom, the cat clinging to his overcoat like grim death. He yanked a bath towel off the heated rack, wrapped it around the animal and tried to dry it off. It shuddered with cold and meowed piteously. After a few more minutes of rubbing, it looked slightly less like a demonic imp from hell. He could see that, although its fur was mostly black, it had white paws like socks. A red leather collar circled its neck: it had to be someone's pet.

"There you go, cat." At long last, he managed to extract its claws from his coat. He set it down on the tiles next to the radiator. Now he had to feed the damn thing.

He made his way to the kitchen. On his way there, he flung off his sodden coat and retrieved his keys and driver's license. I'm going mad, he thought, shivering. Hallucinating. Seeing lions of all things.

He seized the bottle of cognac standing on the granite counter, poured himself a generous shot and downed it.

Alzheimer's at forty-eight, he thought. Rare, but medically possible. Or maybe it's because the wretched Tories got elected by a landslide—that's what's pushed me over the edge.

He faced an unpleasant Executive Committee meeting first thing in the morning. The Assistant Deputy Ministers' formal introduction to the new Minister of Health: a man named Herb Cott, a first-time MPP and an as yet unknown quantity. Amdur's IT staff had scoured the internet and uncovered that Cott's life experience was limited to running a bait shop. In the same riding where the new Premier kept his family cottage, of course.

From selling worms to managing the multi-billion dollar operations of the Ministry of Health. Wonderful! Amdur poured himself another shot of cognac.

"Meow!" The cat had followed him into the kitchen. It crouched on the slate tiles, its luminous green eyes looking up at him expectantly.

Right, feed the damn cat. He set down his empty glass and searched through the cupboards. No tuna, but he did have some canned salmon. It was Nora, his wife's favorite comfort food. Even now with Nora gone, he couldn't resist buying it whenever he made the effort to go grocery shopping.

He opened the can, slopped a few spoonfuls onto a saucer and set it down on the floor. The cat gave it a tentative sniff.

"Salmon not good enough for you?" Amdur opened his stainless steel refrigerator and found a carton of milk. He poured a little milk into a soup bowl and turned to give it to the cat. The salmon had disappeared.

"That was fast work." He set the milk down in front of the cat, fetched a dry bath towel from the bathroom, folded it and put it down in front of the kitchen radiator.

"There's your spot," he told it.

Now for the other end. He glanced at his watch. Already time for the morning paper to be delivered. Given its praise for the Tories' promised deep cuts to health care spending, he couldn't think of a better use for it.

But when he opened the outside door to pick up the paper, he noticed a large shopping bag sitting on the verandah. Inside it he found a plastic litter pan, kitty litter and several cans of cat food.

And a handwritten note that said: I know where you live.

He woke with a start three hours later. The cat had crawled onto the foot of his bed while he slept. It purred as he examined the red leather collar around its neck. No tags, nothing that could identify its owner.

"What am I going to do with you?" he said to the cat as he got ready for work. "No time to find your owner this morning. I'm already fiendishly late."

Despite grabbing a taxi, he was the last of the ADMs to arrive at the Executive Committee Boardroom. Vladimir Nickle, the aged Deputy Minister, raised a sparse eyebrow in disapproval. Amdur's colleagues shouted their ribald greetings, ignoring Nickle as usual. Nickle's lengthy and ineffectual sojourn at the Ministry had allowed them to run their divisions as they pleased—and assured their ongoing loyalty to him.

Amdur tossed out a few cheerful zingers in reply before he dropped into his usual chair beside his friend and ally, Judy Reed, the ADM of Communications and Community Health. A blissful aroma of fresh coffee emanated from the credenza over by the wall, reminding him that he'd missed breakfast. He noticed that Nickle had dusted off the Ministry's official china set and even ordered muffins in honour of Cott's visit.

"Muffins!" Amdur eyed them hungrily. "Nickle never budgets for food. Even at Christmas," he whispered to Judy.

"Cott won't care about Nickle's little party," she whispered back. "My sources tell me the Premier's staff call him The Cutter. He hates all forms of government. In fact, he calls us bureaucrats 'civil serpents'."

"What did we poor overworked government buggers do to him? Turn down his fishing license?"

"Don't joke. The Cutter's catchphrase is: I'm derailing the government gravy train."

"Hardly auspicious."

Amdur glanced at his watch. Minister Cutter and his retinue were already several minutes late. Casual conversations broke out around the table. Nickle appeared to be dozing off.

Since Judy ran a cat rescue service during her meager spare time, Amdur entertained her with the tale of his late night adventures—though he carefully omitted any mention of the lion.

"The way that police officer behaved!" she said. "That poor kitty! His owners must be frantic. You should file a complaint with Toronto Police Services."

"Oh, I can't be bothered. I'll drop the cat off at the Humane Society tonight."

"Well, you could do that, I suppose. But many owners don't think to look there for their lost pets. I know a faster way. Is the cat chipped?"

"You mean a microchip?"

"Yes, vets sometimes put a chip under the cat's skin. It holds the owner's contact information. I know a nice vet in Riverdale. Why don't you take the cat there? Ask him to read your cat's chip."

"Fine, but how do I carry the bloody cat over to the vet clinic? I need a leash or something."

Judy laughed. "I have a spare cat carrier in my office. Drop by and pick it up." She laid a warning hand on his arm. "Heads up."

Nickle's eyes had creaked open. He uttered a dry cough. "Gentlemen, ladies. Time is rather getting on. Have any of you had word...from your respective staffs...that perhaps..."

"Our new guy is wandering around doing an impromptu inspection?" one of the other ADMs filled in.

"Exactly."

A flurry of Blackberries and iPads hit the table. After a lot of furious tapping and hushed conversations, everyone came up empty. No sign of the new minister.

Nickle heaved a windy sigh. "Rather a basic question perhaps, but do we know what our new Minister looks like? He is …um…rather an unknown quantity. Do we perchance have a…um…photograph?"

Glances were exchanged. Amdur pulled up a file on his iPad, quietly blessing his IT staff for covering his backside. "This is him."

He passed his iPad to Nickle who passed it on. It circled the boardroom table to cries of "He's fishing in his canoe, how cute." "People voted for that?" "Who's uglier, him or the pickerel he just caught?"

"Might I have your attention?" Nickle's voice sounded surprisingly strong. "Benjamin, you're the practical one. Would you mind…"

"Of course." Amdur rose and left the boardroom, taking his iPad with him.

Rather than searching aimlessly through the rabbit warren of corridors at Queen's Park, he took the elevator straight down to the main lobby. To his relief one of the senior security guards, Ludmilla, an uncompromising Russian immigrant, sat on duty at the main reception desk.

"Sure, I see this weirdo." She handed him back his iPad. "He say, hey you lady, take me to Minister's office. So I say, sure, no problem, but Minister he is busy guy. You go down hall to Service Ontario. Stand in line for your health card like normal peoples."

Disaster, Amdur thought. He rushed down the hall to the Service Ontario office, looking frantically for signs of the Minister's party. In the crowded room, he spotted no well-tailored people who could be Cott or his aides.

He handed his iPad to the receptionist sitting at the entrance to Service Ontario. She studied the screen and pointed to the waiting area. There in the front row, his back to them, sat a rumpled fiftyish man, alone.

Amdur straightened his posture and walked over to him. It was Cott all right, a scowl on his face and a number slip in his hand.

"Minister Cott?"

Bloodshot eyes stared up at him from under a set of shaggy brows. Cott wore a hunting vest over his red plaid shirt. His stained khaki pants were shoved into a pair of muddy rubber boots. No hat graced his close-cropped head.

"We're waiting for you upstairs, Minister. Is your team with you?"

"Nope."

Cott heaved his bulk out of the chair and followed Amdur out of the Service Ontario office. When they passed security in the main lobby, Cott balled up the paper number and tossed it in Ludmilla's face.

Amdur cleared his throat in protest, but Cott had already barreled over to the elevators. They continued their journey upstairs in deathly silence.

When they reached the top floor, Amdur ushered Cott down the hall into the Executive Boardroom. None of the ADMs could conceal their surprise. The pickerel had landed.

Nickle creaked to his feet and offered Cott his chair. Cott plunked himself down and said nothing. He made a slow study of each of the ADMs in turn.

A staring contest, Amdur realized, annoyed at Cott's childish power game. He watched Nickle teeter over to the credenza, pour out a cup of coffee and shakily set it down in front of the new Minister.

Cott looked at it. "What's that? You trying to poison me?"

Nickle uttered a dry laugh. "Good joke, Minister. Very good joke." He signaled to the others to join in the laughter. No one did.

"Go sit over there." Cott pointed Nickle to the chairs along the side of the room where his aides, had they been there, were supposed to sit. Nickle shrugged and did as he was told.

Cott leaned his burly forearms on the boardroom table. "Now then. Your Ministry eats up thirty billion dollars every single year. Your Ministry eats up more'n any other goddamn government department. Hell, it eats up more'n all them departments combined. That's money you guys steal right out of the taxpayer's wallet."

"With respect, Minister, Ontario taxpayers do get considerable benefits from our health care system," Amdur put in.

"Oh, you think so, eh? I'll tell you what the taxpayers want. They want choice. They don't want no nanny state. They want their freedom back."

"You mean freedom to die if you can't afford a doctor or a hospital," Judy said from her place next to Amdur.

Cott ignored her. "Now you all listen up good. No more swimming around in gravy. I'm cutting your health budget by fifty percent. That's right: fifty percent. That's what I told the voters I'd do when I got elected and you're gonna watch me do it. Next year, I'm cutting you buggers back another fifty percent. You wanna keep working here, you'll do what I say. Understand?"

In the stunned silence that followed, Cott foraged in his hunting vest for a cigar. He leaned back, clumped his muddy feet on the mahogany table and lit up.

"Minister, the…um…presentations," Nickle ventured from his exile next to the muffins.

"Save it. I'm gonna meet with each and every one of you." Cott pointed with his cigar. "And each of you is gonna have to prove to me why I don't just axe you and your whole damn department." He swayed forward, thumping his feet on the floor. "And in case any of you civil serpents get any ideas, remember: Herb Cott stabs from the front."

"No problem, Minister," Amdur couldn't help saying. "I believe you've come to the right place."

"You certainly didn't help matters," Judy said later that afternoon when Amdur dropped by her office to pick up the cat carrier.

"Sorry." Amdur slumped into the chair facing her desk. "The world's gone mad. A fool of a worm seller bent on destroying the health system of fourteen million people."

"I know." She wiped her nose with a tissue.

"Good heavens, Judy. You've been crying."

"Close the door." While he did so, she opened the bottom drawer of her desk and pulled out a bottle of scotch and two glasses. "Join me?"

"Of course." He watched her pour out two generous shots. "What's happened?"

"Cott was just here. He accused me and my division of handing out freebies to illegal immigrants and perverts. He's closing down all the walk-in clinics in the province, starting with the AIDS clinics."

"That's illegal. He'll never get away with it."

"The Tories have a majority in the House. They can do whatever they like. The Cabinet will simply pass an executive order. They could do it tonight."

Amdur took a large swallow of scotch. Crazy as it sounded, Judy was right.

"It's not the money, Ben. Mother and I will manage somehow. But if Cott fires me or I quit my job, who will fight for the AIDS clinics? He's flushing thirty years of progress down the drain."

"We *all* have to fight Cott. All the ADMs together."

"We'll all be fighting too hard to protect our own turfs. You know how it works."

Maybe we're not civil serpents as much as rats, Amdur thought.

"Cott's a horrible, petty little man." Judy swiped at her nose. "He's cancelled all vacations until further notice. Everyone in the Ministry has to work through Christmas. If he fires you, he's making you work the mandatory two week notice period. And that includes Christmas, of course. Lay-offs start tomorrow. He bragged about it!"

"That bastard!" Amdur drained his glass. "No one takes my staff without a fight."

But he knew he was facing the battle of his life.

The cat was waiting by the front door when Amdur returned home that night. It purred loudly and rubbed itself against his legs.

"Well, cat, you're the only happy person I've seen today."

He made for the kitchen and heard it patter in after him. While he heated up a frozen dinner in the microwave, he opened one of the cans of cat food the police officer had left him.

"Disgusting muck." Amdur stared at the can's contents and refilled the cat's dish. "Like pate that's gone off. But you seem to like it well enough."

The cat made a strange humming noise while it ate, purring and chewing at the same time.

He poured out milk for the cat and a large glass of Bordeaux for himself. When his dinner was ready, he carried it into his study and set it down on the desk next to his laptop. With all the day's distractions, he faced hours of more work before bed.

I've got to put a stop to The Cutter, but how? he thought. I can't even trust my own brain. Did I see that wretched lion or didn't I?

He gulped down his meal while he combed the internet for reports of escaped lions in Toronto. Nothing. Frustrated, he pulled out his Blackberry and dialed Toronto Police Services. After an excruciating maze of telephone menus, he reached the duty officer.

"No sir, no reports about lions missing from the Toronto Zoo. Are you quite sure that's what you saw?"

Time to track down the cat-throwing police officer, Amdur decided. Filing a complaint would make him feel better.

He told the duty officer what had happened.

"Did she give you her name and badge number?"

"No, I forgot to ask."

"Sir, the force has over five thousand sworn officers. And a lot of them are dark-haired females in their twenties."

"Surely to God you know the names of the officers on patrol in Riverdale last night!"

"Sure do. Constables Gupta and Chan. Both male. Have yourself a nice night, sir."

Amdur was left listening to the dial tone. Wonderful, he thought. Now the police have me down on their weirdo list.

"Meow!" The cat appeared next to his chair. In the next instant, it leaped onto his desk and knocked over his wine glass.

"Damn it, cat." He wiped up the wine. "Never mind. Time for me to get to work." The cat stretched out across his keyboard. "Enough foolishness." He lifted the cat onto his lap where it settled down. More purring.

It stayed put while Amdur quenched the critical issues burning in his division. At the same time, he tried to reassure his staff that the Ministry wasn't going down like the Titanic.

Ha, bloody ha, he thought.

At midnight an urgent e-mail appeared in his inbox. Nickle had resigned his post as deputy minister.

Amdur leaned back, absently stroking the cat. "Poor Nickle. What a cold-hearted Merry Christmas after forty-five years of service! Inevitable, I suppose." He sighed. "Tell me, cat, what did you see last night? Did *you* see the lion?"

The cat looked up attentively. Its pointed black and white face was rather sweet, Amdur thought.

"I can't just keep calling you 'cat'. All right, while you're staying with me, why don't I call you Tiddles? That's the name of my wife, Nora's cat, the one she grew up with. He was quite the character apparently. I used to enjoy her stories about Tiddles. You see, I never had pets as a child. Too difficult in central London, especially with both parents working as doctors."

Amdur roused himself. It wouldn't do to get attached to the cat. It belonged with its owners, whoever they were.

He searched out the website of the vet clinic Judy had recommended. It opened early in the morning. He'd have just enough time to drop by with Tiddles before work.

The Saint Francis Animal Hospital sat on Parliament Street a short distance down from Peepers, Riverdale's notorious strip club.

At least the strippers have some Christmas spirit, Amdur thought as he lugged the cat carrier past the club to the vet clinic. Red and green lights were ablaze in its garish marquee, and massive Christmas wreaths adorned its tarnished brass doors.

He and Tiddles were the animal hospital's first customers. A tiny dark man in medical greens introduced himself as the veterinarian, Dr. Ali.

"Muhammad Ali, actually," the vet said as he showed them into the examination room. "This is a big joke, yes?"

Amdur cracked a smile. He set the cat carrier down on the steel examining table and tried to extricate Tiddles. The cat had resisted getting into the carrier and now only a nuclear bomb could dislodge him.

"Allow me." Dr. Ali dug some cat treats out of his jacket pocket. They worked like magic. Tiddles emerged and, in short order, allowed himself to be examined. "How long have you owned your kitty?"

Amdur explained that he'd found Tiddles in Riverdale Park.

"I see. Well, your lost kitty is a neutered male. Looking at his teeth, I would say he is about five years old." The vet ran his gentle hands down Tiddles' sides. "He is rather thin, but his coat is thick. I would agree with you, doctor, that he is somebody's pet. He has a lovely nature, but...he is nervous. Has he suffered a trauma?"

"A predator chased him. A li—." Amdur stopped himself just in time.

"Exactly! Coyotes and foxes travel down the ravine system to hunt in our city. The outdoors is dangerous for kitties." He fingered the scruff of Tiddles' neck. "Good news. The kitty has a chip. I will read it and try to locate his owner."

He picked up Tiddles and carried him through the connecting door of the examination room into the innards of the animal hospital.

Alone for the moment, Amdur called his executive assistant, Lesley Wong, on his Blackberry.

"So far no earth-shattering crises—or at least they can wait till you get here," she told him. "Oh, and Otto Winter, your IT security consultant, wants to see you."

Wonderful, Amdur thought. Otto never asked for a meeting unless his IT crisis *was* earth-shattering. "Very well. Tell Otto I'll see him for lunch at my usual pub." He couldn't afford the time to eat lunch, but now he couldn't afford not to.

He finished the call just as Dr. Ali returned with Tiddles.

"I have good news and bad news," the vet said. "The good news is that I have located the kitty's owner."

"And the bad news?"

"I have spoken with her. She lives in Mississauga."

"But how could Tiddles end up in Riverdale Park? He'd have to cross thirty kilometers of highways and busy city streets to get here."

"Exactly. Sad to say some cat owners are not good people. When they no longer want their kitty, they simply throw him away. In a park or a cemetery."

"I can't return Tiddles to that woman. She'll only dump him somewhere else."

"True enough. Luckily, she does not want him back. But she did say a strange thing. She claims he ran away in June. Obviously he has not been living rough for six months. He has found a new home in this area. This is the owner you must locate."

Amdur's heart sank. "What do you suggest?"

"My staff will put up a notice. That sometimes works. And you might call the other vet clinics near here."

Amdur thought hard for a moment. "Tell me, do you know of an animal hospital that deals with, um, much larger animals?"

"Do you mean horses? Or farm animals?"

"No, I meant…a lion."

"A lion?" Dr. Ali laughed, highly amused. "Heavens, no! To own such a beast in downtown Toronto would be highly illegal. Why do you ask?"

"Oh…er… curiosity." The ring of his Blackberry saved him from further explanation. He recognized Judy Reed's name on the call display. She sounded panic-stricken when he answered.

"I just stepped out to call you. Cott and his crew are in my office. They're coming to see you next. And, Ben, Cott is on the warpath."

No time to take Tiddles home. Amdur quickly paid the vet clinic and hailed a cab outside. While the taxi tore down Wellesley Street to Queen's Park, he phoned Lesley, his executive assistant, to warn her about Cott's imminent arrival.

"Take the freight elevator. I'll meet you," she said. "Judy will try to stall them another five minutes."

When he got to Queen's Park, Ludmilla, the security guard, unlocked the freight elevator for him and sent him and Tiddles up to his floor.

Lesley was waiting for him when he arrived. He tore off his overcoat and gloves and handed them to her. But when he tried to give her the cat carrier, she waved it away, eyes and nose streaming.

"I can't, Ben. Allergies…"

He could hear Cott's rough voice approaching. No time. He ran into his office, sat down behind his desk and shoved Tiddles' carrier beneath it.

"No noise, Tiddles." He had only seconds to fire up his iPad before Cott burst into his office with two men behind him.

The first, a tall bulky man, closed Amdur's door and took up position in front of it. Obviously a private bodyguard. The other much smaller, thinner man set down his briefcase and introduced himself as Cott's lawyer.

Both of Cott's aides wore expensive suits. Perhaps that was why The Cutter had switched his hunting gear for a dusty blue blazer over a golf shirt. Muddy Doc Martins replaced his rubber boots. He sat down in the visitor's chair opposite Amdur's desk without asking. The lawyer stayed on his feet.

"You've got a lot of computer types in your shop," Cott said without preamble. "You can tell 'em their jobs are going. Over to India where they do the same stuff for cheap."

"I regret, Minister, that simply won't be possible," Amdur said.

"What's your problem? Look at you. You're from there and you're working here."

"I'm a Canadian citizen via England." Amdur breathed deeply to stay calm. "And Minister, you cannot replace a Canadian's job with a foreign national. It's against the law."

"Corporations ship jobs offshore all the time. Hell, one of the big banks just did it."

"And got in a lot of trouble for it."

"So what? Get used to idea. And fast." Cott pulled out a cigar and pointed it at the lawyer. "You, fix it."

The lawyer coughed discreetly. "With all due respect, Minister. Dr. Amdur does have a point."

"He does, does he?" Cott lit up.

"Would you mind putting that out?" Amdur said. "My executive assistant is extremely allergic to tobacco smoke."

"She's not here."

"She will be in my office after you leave."

Cott scowled. The lawyer plucked the smoldering cigar from his fingers and walked it over to the security guard, who took it outside.

"Where's he going? I need my protection," Cott said.

"He'll only be gone a moment," the lawyer assured him. "In the meantime, we have that other more serious issue to discuss."

At that moment, Tiddles let out an unearthly howl from where he sat trapped in the cat carrier.

"What the hell was that?" Cott looked around frantically.

"Nothing." Amdur folded his hands on top of the desk. "Did you hear anything?" he asked the lawyer.

"Um…not sure. The issue, Minister?"

"Oh, yeah." Cott collected himself. "You got a criminal working for you. In security no less. Now *that's* gotta be illegal."

"Ah, you must mean Otto Winter," Amdur said "He's our security expert. And yes, he does have a suspended sentence for computer hacking. An old sentence, I'd like to point out. He's saved Ontario taxpayers tens of millions of dollars by tracking down health care fraud."

"So what? Fire him."

"I can't."

"Can't or won't?"

"Both. I refuse to fire an excellent member of my staff without cause. And may I point out, Minister, I'm sure you don't want a lawsuit for unfair dismissal on your hands."

Cott looked at his lawyer. "Can the Winter guy do that?"

"I'm afraid so, Minister," the lawyer said.

"Bull crap. He don't have the bucks to sue." Cott leaned forward, pointing. "Now you listen to me…"

Tiddles let out another anguished howl. Cott froze, index finger in midair. "You…you've got a cat in here. A cat!"

"I'm sure he doesn't, Minister." The lawyer threw a worried glance at Amdur. "You don't, do you?"

Busted, Amdur thought. "Actually, I do. Tiddles is our divisional house cat. I find that he's good for employee morale. And improved productivity."

"Protection…where's my protection?" Cott's pudgy features took on a strange purplish hue. "He's killing me…I can't breathe."

Amdur leaped up to intervene, worried that The Cutter had a bad heart, but the lawyer waved him off and helped Cott to his feet.

"Herb, it's OK. We're going, OK? And Amdur is going to get rid of the damn cat. Right?"

"As you wish."

Wheezing, Cott leaned on Amdur's desk. "You…you planned this. You tried to kill me. You're dead…you hear me? You're dead."

He shook off his lawyer's helping hand and stumbled out of Amdur's office. The lawyer shrugged, picked up his briefcase and followed him.

Amdur sank back into his chair. "Well, Tiddles, I believe we've witnessed the worst case of felinophobia I've ever seen. And now since I've been declared dead, I am going to lunch."

A biting wind tore down Bay Street, chilling Amdur as he walked south with Tiddles to his favorite pub, The Duke of Somerset. The hostess smiled when she recognized him and turned a blind eye to the cat carrier. She led him to his usual booth at the back where a fat sixtyish man sat nursing a glass of foamy beer.

Amdur slid into the booth opposite Otto Winter. He put the cat carrier on the bench, its mesh gate facing him so he could keep an eye on Tiddles.

"New friend, doctor? Personally I prefer the ladies." Otto grinned over his beer. His cropped grey hair and stubbly jowls reminded Amdur of a decayed storm trooper.

"Never mind the cat. What's the problem?"

"Better get your beer first. You will need it." Otto groped through his grubby back pack and heaved a battered laptop onto the table.

Amdur ordered a much-needed pint of Boddingtons ale. It arrived in a flash and he took a grateful swallow. "All right, how bad is the bad news?"

"Our new dictator, Cott the Cutter, tried to hack into your email. Indeed he tried to explore the confidential files of your entire division."

"What!"

"Not to worry. No one gets through my firewalls. But Cott certainly has been a busy little beaver."

"But Cott's an idiot worm salesman. He can't be doing the hacking himself."

"Of course not. His lawyer hired a computer rat in Asia to do Cott's dirty work. A sneaky little rat, but sadly for him, not a deep thinker. I amused myself a little, then boom! I spiked him. For me, a piece of delicious cake."

Otto finished his beer and fished a rumpled envelope from the pocket of his equally rumpled jacket. "My resignation."

"Over my dead body!" Amdur banged down his beer glass. "The Ministry needs you. Now more than ever."

Otto shrugged his heavy shoulders. "You may change your mind in a minute. You see, last night after I fixed the rat, I made a wormhole in Cott's firewall. And up periscope!" He twisted his index finger to demonstrate.

"I shouldn't be hearing this."

"Even your cat could breach Cott's el-cheapo security. Relax, doctor. No one detected my ghost in The Cutter's infernal machine." Otto laced his fingers over his ample paunch. "Now ask me anything."

"Otto, I'm going to pretend this conversation never happened."

"I knew you would have scruples. Too bad." Otto nudged his resignation letter over to Amdur's side of the table. "Cott spends all his time on line watching porno."

"How depressingly predictable!"

"Allow me to share the kinky details over lunch. My parting gift to the Ministry."

Otto fired up his laptop.

Otto's resignation letter in his pocket, Amdur flagged down a cab after lunch and took Tiddles home. While the taxi waited outside, he released the cat from his carrier and refilled his dishes. Poor Tiddles, he thought as he gave him a pat, you've had a tough day. But then again, haven't we all?

The darkening skies matched his mood as the cab returned him to Queen's Park. Ludmilla barely acknowledged him when he passed by the reception desk. No doubt after her run-in with Cott, she was working her two week notice through Christmas.

Back on his floor, he found Lesley stripping the ornaments off the office Christmas tree.

"Cott just cancelled all staff Christmas parties," she said. "All decorations are to be taken down. Not work-related he says, that SOB."

"Leave the tree up. Put the decorations back on. I'll deal with Cott and his boys personally if they bother us about it."

"Thanks, Ben. I could use some Christmas cheer right now."

"And we're throwing a farewell party for Nickle tomorrow morning. Here in my office. Call the caterers, send me the bill. Invite the whole damn Ministry."

"I'll get right on it. And never mind the caterers. We all do potluck at Christmas."

I've got to neutralize Cott, but how? Amdur thought. For the rest of the day he tried to focus on work, but his mind teemed with the unwanted images of Cott's sex fantasies that Otto had shared over lunch: Cott dressed as an anime school girl, spanking parties, dominatrixes…

He didn't shut down his laptop until the cleaning staff arrived outside his office. He decided to walk home though it was well past midnight. Maybe the frosty air would clear his head.

When he reached Parliament Street, he thought of the vet clinic. Had Dr. Ali's staff put up a notice about Tiddles? Might as well check since he was here.

Business at Peepers strip club was brisk. Its brass doors stood open despite the chill, a crowd of patrons smoking outside. The loud throb of pop music assailed his ears as he passed under the pulsating lights of its marquee. Weaving his way around the smokers, something caught his eye.

He stopped in the middle of the sidewalk and stared.

I've been had!

Directly across the street from Peepers stood a Lebanese café. Thankfully it was still open. Amdur nabbed a seat by the front window where he had a full view of Peepers' brass doors. Shortly after he polished off his falafel, he spotted her leaving.

She strolled a short distance up Parliament and turned onto Winchester, the same street where he'd fled the lion two nights before.

He left the café and chased after her.

She seemed preoccupied. All to the good since he was a complete novice at spying. He kept pace half a block behind her, dodging the recycling bins set out for next day's waste collection.

At the end of Winchester, she veered north onto Sumach Street. He raced to the corner only to find that she'd vanished. He swore in frustration.

The ground floor lights of the corner house flashed on—the same house where he'd stood watching the lion. Did she live *there*?

He remembered holding onto the black iron fence that encircled the house's front garden. But its back garden lay hidden by a high brick wall. Interesting…

He heard an outside door squeak open. And a voice, unmistakably hers, speaking in warm, affectionate tones.

"Did you miss me, Cyrano? Did you, baby?"

He had to see into that garden. He seized a nearby recycling bin and wheeled it over to the brick wall. In an ungainly scramble, he heaved himself onto the bin's lid. Leaning on his knees, he grasped the top of the rough brick wall and looked down into the garden.

And saw the lion!

He frolicked in the snow like an oversized dog. When she called his name, he bounded up to her and rubbed his huge mane against the navy legs of her police uniform.

"Good evening," Amdur called down from his perch. "Now I know where *you* live."

The lion turned. His yellow eyes gleamed, a ridge of the fur bristled down his back. He let out an unearthly roar that rattled nearby windows.

"Cyrano, no!" she shouted.

The lion crouched, ready to spring. Amdur lost his balance. In an explosion of noise, he flew off the recycling bin and crashed down onto the icy sidewalk. He stared at the stars, winded, unable to move. Waiting for the dread dark shape of the carnivore to leap over the wall.

He heard her anxious voice call: "Cyrano! Cyrano!" Followed by the lion's roars and grunts as it loped back and forth on the other side of the wall.

Got to get out of here…got to. Before it jumps over and gets me.

His right knee hurt like a bastard. He rolled onto his side and dragged himself up.

Got to get home.

He limped down to the street corner. Now to get past the lion's house.

He heard the front door bang open.

"Wait, wait! Are you all right?" She charged down the verandah steps to intercept him.

He waved her off. "I'll be fine. Just keep that bloodthirsty animal of yours locked up. Now get out of my way. I've had a bloody awful day."

"Please don't call the police."

"Why not? You impersonated a police officer. And you're keeping a dangerous predator in a neighbourhood full of children."

"Cyrano's a sweetheart. He's completely tame. And I never said I was a cop."

"You led me on—admit it."

"All right, yes, I did. But I was desperate. I had to save Cyrano. The police would have shot him on sight."

Amdur couldn't argue with that. "He was behind the bushes the other night, wasn't he?"

"Yes, but he would never have hurt you. He's gentle and affectionate. Why don't you come in and see for yourself? I put him back in his cage. You'll be safe, I swear."

"To find out first hand if he likes human flesh? No, thank you!"

"At least tell me if Boots is all right."

"You mean the poor cat you threw at me? Obviously he's yours, too. Or was. Well, he's my cat now. And his name is Tiddles."

She started to cry. "I'm sorry. I'm so, so sorry. I didn't know what else to do. I had to get you out of the park before anyone else saw Cyrano. And-and now I've lost Boots…Tiddles…"

"At least he won't end up as an aperitif for Cyrano."

"NO! Cyrano would never hurt him. They're best friends. Look, Cyrano and I are going back to Las Vegas in a couple of days. I landed a six month gig. Can we please talk about this?"

"Fine." And so, against all his better instincts, Amdur gave in.

Sophie—for that was her name—settled him in the spacious kitchen at the back of the corner house. She placed an ice pack on his knee and a glass of bourbon in his hand.

Cyrano crouched in a cage-like structure that resembled an oversized dog crate. He threw off a fusty, gamy odour that filled the room—indeed the entire house. The corner mansion, Amdur learned, belonged to Sophie's aunt who'd moved into a retirement home.

"I miss Boots," she said, wiping her eyes. "I found him in the park last June. He was starving, I nursed him back to health."

"You mean to say that you and Cyrano have been living in Riverdale for *six months!*"

She nodded. "We were between jobs."

"That cage looks flimsy." Amdur and Cyrano glowered at each other. "Small wonder he got out."

"It's my fault. Cyrano gets so bored cooped up in his cage. I let him have free run of the house sometimes. He's never caused trouble before. The other night I forgot to lock the front door. So he got out. Boots, too. Cyrano knows how to work door knobs. He's very intelligent."

As if on cue, the lion emitted a low vibrating growl.

"You hear that? He's purring." She refilled Amdur's glass. "I raised him from a cub. My folks, well, we're all circus people." She sighed. "I suppose you saw my photo outside Peepers."

"Yes, Sergeant Cupid, I did. Your police officer act is very convincing."

"I'm not ashamed. Pole dancing keeps me in shape. And it costs a lot to feed Cyrano." She frowned. "So are you going to turn me in?"

Amdur sighed. It was Christmas after all. "Fine, I keep Tiddles. You keep Cyrano. But first you're going to help me with something. We're going to turn the worms in Ontario's biggest bait shop!"

"I'm an ADM in the Ontario government's largest ministry. I can't believe I let you talk me into this." Judy's hands danced along the rim of her van's steering wheel. Their wait at the Bay Street intersection outside Queen's Park was proving endless.

"Sorry about the short notice," Amdur said from the passenger seat. "You're the only one I could trust." His stomach burned. He'd worked through the night, fueled by endless espressos—and now this. "This was *not* part of the plan, believe me."

Behind them, Cyrano yawned, bathing them in sulfurous breath. At least a sturdy metal grille separated him from driver and passenger.

Sophie snickered from where she sat beside her lion. "Cyrano's just a big pussy cat, aren't you, big boy?"

Judy coughed. "I can't believe this. Driving a lion through morning rush hour traffic. In my cat rescue van. A lion!"

"I already told your buddy, Amdur, here. I can't leave Cyrano alone. He nearly got out again last night. Where I go, he goes. Or the deal's off."

"What deal?"

"The less you know about it, the better," Amdur put in.

"Ben, whatever you're planning, drop it. There are a thousand ways this will screw up. And you, Sophie, you should be thrown off the police force. We'll all end up in jail. This will kill Mother."

"No one is going to jail." Amdur wished he could feel more certain about that. "And Sophie's not a cop. She's a stripper."

"Oh, God." Judy leaned her forehead on the steering wheel. "I'm losing it."

"No, you are not losing it. Breathe deep. In, out." Amdur rested his hand on her back. "Come on now, in and out. You've faced down coyotes attacking lost cats. You can do this."

"Green light!" Sophie cried.

Horns blared behind them. Judy tromped on the accelerator. Amdur crashed back against his seat as they tore across the intersection.

Cyrano's claws scrabbled for purchase on the metal floor. He let out a bellow of fear. Sophie yelled and dragged on his chain.

The van swerved left, fish tailed down into darkness and slammed to a halt. Amdur hit the dash. Somehow, miraculously, Judy had steered them into the underground parking garage.

"Are you crazy!" Sophie shouted. "Cyrano get down! Cyrano!"

The lion let out an ear-shattering roar. Judy's screams matched his.

"Shut up! Shut up or this whole thing is off!" Sophie shouted.

"Everyone calm down!" Heart thumping, Amdur groped through the glove box and yanked out Judy's secret stash of scotch. "You, drink this." Judy seized the bottle, tore off the cap and sucked on it like oxygen. "And you, Sophie, control that bloody animal!"

Sophie glared at him. Cyrano moved restlessly, clinking his chain. They waited in strained silence until after a long huff, the lion dropped back down.

"We're wasting precious time." Amdur checked his Blackberry. "All right, Otto has turned off the security cameras. Down to the freight bay."

"OK." Judy shoved the scotch bottle between her knees. She restarted the van and drove down to the next level.

They pulled into the deserted cargo bay. Ludmilla appeared on the loading platform.

Sophie gasped. "A cop!"

"It's all right. She's one of us." He acknowledged Ludmilla's thumbs-up. "Sophie and I are off now. Be ready to roll when I text you." Amdur gave Judy's arm a squeeze. "Remember: we're saving the health care of fourteen million people."

"Fine, just leave me the scotch." Judy clutched the bottle to her chest.

Amdur jumped out of the van. He slid back the side door to release Sophie and Cyrano.

The lion sniffed the air, wrinkling his face at the smell of exhaust and gasoline. At Sophie's command he leaped onto the landing of the cargo bay. Amdur and Sophie followed him by way of the stairs.

Ludmilla gave Cyrano the once-over. "Nice lion. Beautiful animal. You feed him today, little girl?"

"He's perfectly tame!"

"Too bad. Maybe he change his mind when he sees Cott's fat ass."

She unlocked the freight elevator door with a grin. Amdur, Sophie and Cyrano climbed aboard. The door closed in front of them with a loud clang. The elevator lurched into motion, heading toward the top floor and the minister's office.

"Got your iPhone?" he asked Sophie. "Let's run through things one more time."

"Leave it! I know what to do." She frowned. "After today, we're done. Forever."

"Agreed."

"If this screws up, I won't be the only one going to jail. That's a promise."

"It'll be worth it." Amdur checked his phone. The message read: "Meeting full."

"What meeting?" Sophie read his screen without apology.

"It means we're safe for the moment. Everyone on the top floor is gone."

"Gone where?"

"To the farewell Christmas party for Vladimir Nickle, our old deputy minister. In my office, next floor down." The elevator bumped to a stop. "Here we are."

The doors rolled open. Faint sounds from Nickle's party trickled up the emergency stairwell to their left.

Amdur put the freight elevator on hold. He moved down to the end of the hallway and looked round the corner. The empty main corridor stretched down to the glass security barrier fronting the Minister's office. Outside it stood Cott's bodyguard.

"Damn!"

"What's going on?" Sophie pressed up behind him with a rattle of Cyrano's chain.

"Cott's bodyguard is still here."

"I'll take care of him. You hold Cyrano." She handed Amdur the leash. "Baby, lie down. I'll be back soon."

The lion grunted and sprawled on the floor. Sophie straightened her police uniform and strolled down to the Minister's office.

The bodyguard didn't speak until she reached the glass barrier. "Something wrong, officer?" Without the normal background office noise, his voice carried.

"Yes, I have an urgent message for Minister Cott from the Premier's office," Sophie said.

"OK, I'll give it to him."

"No can do. A Christmas card. From the Tory party. It's personal."

"Oh, right." The guard sounded weary. "I get it. That kind of Christmas card."

"We need some privacy, say fifteen minutes. Can you fix that?"

"Yeah, I guess."

Amdur listened to the man's footsteps retreat. A heartbeat later he heard the swoosh of the main elevator doors.

Cyrano howled and leaped up, jerking the lead out of Amdur's grip. He loped down the corridor with Amdur in pursuit. Sophie was halfway through the security barrier.

She stopped, propping up the door with her foot. "You were supposed to hold him!"

"He got away from me."

"Fine, he can come visit the big bad boss." She picked up the lion's chain.

"NO!" Amdur said in a hoarse whisper. "Cott has a cat phobia. If he sees Cyrano, he'll have a heart attack."

"I thought that was the idea. Fine, take Cyrano in there." She pointed to the women's washroom directly opposite to where they were standing. "And don't upset him." She tossed him the lion's lead. "Cyrano, walkies!"

Cyrano whimpered as she disappeared into the Minister's office. Amdur hauled on his chain. By the time he'd dragged the lion into the washroom and shut the door, his arms throbbed with pain.

"Stay there!" Cyrano took shelter under the row of sinks, his tail lashing. Heart thumping, Amdur checked his phone. No messages. The two of them glared at each other.

Five minutes passed.

Sophie bragged she could handle any man. He hoped she was right. He creaked open the washroom door and peered out. Not a sound escaped the Minister's office.

Cyrano bristling mane bumped against his leg. "Stay there. Don't come near me." The lion curled his flaccid blue upper lip and bared his teeth.

His phone went off with a shrill cry. Judy's name appeared on the screen.

"Ben, what's happening?" Her words sounded slurred. "I'm going crazy down here. The media people, they're already…"

Cyrano let out a low growl. It did not sound like purring.

"Shut up, you! No, not you, Judy."

His phone pinged. A message. He cut Judy off.

One word: "Help."

"Sophie!"

I can think of a thousand ways this could go wrong…

He sent an urgent text to Otto for the code to the security door.

Five more minutes passed. No reply.

Another message: "Help!"

Desperate now, he thought of the fire alarm.

"Cyrano, get up! Help, Sophie. Come on, get up!" He tugged on the lion's chain.

He may as well have been reading Cyrano the ministry's annual report. The lion merely yawned and rested his massive head on his front paws.

"You miserable waste of space! Well, bloody stay there!" He dropped the chain and burst out of the washroom. Where the hell was the fire alarm?

"Help!" A scream from the Minister's office.

"Sophie!" He ran over to the barrier. Banged on the glass. Cyrano, trapped in the washroom, let out an echoing roar.

Two figures burst through the Minister's door. A police officer, her uniform torn open, revealing sexy red underwear. And a bulky man in a Japanese schoolgirl uniform brandishing a riding crop. Cott's pale hairy buttocks and drooping appendage were a sight that seared into one's memory.

"Open it! Open up!" Sophie crashed her fists against the glass door.

Amdur, powerless to help, shouted: "I see you, Cott. There's a witness."

Cott seized Sophie by the throat. "Gimme that phone, you bitch!"

Sophie tried to knee him in the crotch and missed.

Several things happened at once. The main elevator doors flew open and released a staggering Judy. Sophie thumped Cott in the eye. And Cyrano flew out of the washroom with a terrifying roar.

He leaped onto the security barrier. His forepaws hung over the top edge. His powerful hind legs scrabbled on the glass pane.

Otto, for God's sake!

Numbers appeared on Amdur's phone screen. He punched the code into the keypad. Tore open the security door.

Sophie burst free. Cott rushed after her, waving the riding crop. Amdur stuck out his foot. Cott tripped and fell. "Gimme that phone." He scrabbled after Sophie.

Amdur kicked the security door shut, cutting off Cott's escape.

A slithering sound. Cyrano glided down from the glass barrier. He bounded toward them.

Cott let out an unearthly shriek of pure terror.

"No, Cyrano! No!" Sophie grabbed for his chain.

Cyrano's paw lashed through the air. Cott tumbled to the floor. The lion stood over him, drooling...

Sophie threw herself at Cyrano. Buried her face in his mane. Stroked his flanks.

"The media. They're here. They're on their way up." Judy choked out. "That's what I tried to tell you."

The lion's pink tongue spilled over his vile-looking fangs. He let out a woof, reluctant to abandon Cott's fat ass.

Sophie murmured to him. After what seemed like an eternity, Cyrano stepped away from Cott's trembling form.

"Get out of here! Run, Judy!" Amdur pushed her in the direction of the freight elevator. "Sophie, get that animal moving."

"Cyrano, gallop!"

Sophie dashed down the corridor. The lion streaked after her in a four-footed animal run.

The main elevators pinged. The doors opened. A full media crew poured out for the Minister's press conference, lights and video cameras at the ready.

Cott staggered up, his garish makeup hideous under his curly blond wig. He saw the reporters and screamed.

"Minister?"

Amdur beat a hasty retreat back down the corridor. A clamor of voices rose behind him. No time to stop. Back at the freight elevator, he turned the key and got it moving.

"Are you all right?"

Sophie nodded. She finished buttoning up her tunic and handed him her phone. "I want that back. And this never happened."

"Fair enough. Give me the keys to the van, Judy. You're in no condition to drive." She handed them over.

The elevator stopped. Ludmilla opened the door and signaled they were still in the clear.

He passed Judy's keys to Sophie. "Leave the van outside my place. You know where I live."

"Where are you going?"

"To Nickle's farewell Christmas party." He closed the elevator doors.

Back upstairs, he and Judy were engulfed by a crowd of partying civil serpents. They spilled out of Amdur's office, occupying every cubicle on the floor. Even Vladimir Nickle had abandoned his crusty sense of decorum. Surrounded by well-wishers, he gulped wine from a plastic glass, his Santa hat askew.

"I'm drunk," Judy whispered.

"No worries. So is everyone else."

Amdur located Otto by the buffet table. Potluck at the Ministry never failed to provide a feast: Otto's paper plate was folded in half under the weight of food.

"I especially recommend the lasagna, doctor."

"Here." Amdur slipped him Sophie's phone.

"Be back, one minute." Otto set down his plate and disappeared.

Amdur turned his attention to the wine table for a much-needed drink. He filled plates with food for him and Judy. A moment later, someone let out a shout by the window.

"Look! Some weirdo's running down Bay Street. There's a TV crew after him."

People crowded to that side of the room.

"Holy shit! It's Cott!" A man stood staring at his phone.

"He's on the government website, too!" A woman pointed to the computer beside her.

Phones and computer screens flashed on, food and wine temporarily forgotten. In the ensuing shock and awe, Otto returned and passed Sophie's phone back to Amdur.

"How did you do that?"

"Oh, a global internet tour via Mauritius. Untraceable. Better you should not ask, doctor." Otto helped himself to Christmas cake.

On Christmas night, Amdur settled back in his study, a glass of cognac in his hand and Tiddles on his lap, to watch his favorite holiday movie, *It's a Wonderful Life*. It certainly is, he thought. This is the best Christmas I've had in years.

The news story of Cott's resignation still had legs two weeks later. The video showcasing his misadventures had millions of hits on websites round the world. American comedy shows trumpeted his antics with actors dressed up as moose and beavers. For once Canadians weren't boring.

Amdur gave Tiddles a pat, happily digesting the Christmas dinner he'd enjoyed earlier with Judy and her mother. On the mantle over the fireplace stood two postcards, one showing a glittering burlesque show in Las Vegas, the other a beach in Mauritius.

Snowflakes drifted slowly past the windows of his flat. And if he stared long and hard enough into Riverdale Park, he imagined they formed the dancing figure of a lion.

About M.H. (Madeleine) Callway

In 2013, Madeleine founded the Mesdames of Mayhem, a collective of established Canadian crime fiction writers. *Thirteen* is the Mesdames' first anthology of crime stories.

Madeleine holds postgraduate degrees in science and business. She worked for many years in public health where she investigated disease outbreaks and exposure to toxic chemicals.

In 2012, her story, *The Lizard*, won the Bony Pete prize sponsored by Bloody Words. It will appear soon in *Crimespree Magazine*. Madeleine's short story, *Incompetence Kills*, appeared in *EFD1: Starship Goodwords*.

Her debut novel, *Gunning for Bear*, was short-listed for the 2012 Unhanged Arthur award and under another title, for the 2009 Debut Dagger award. It will be published by Seraphim Editions in 2014.

Madeleine has taken part in the Toronto Ride to Conquer Cancer every year since its inception.

Connect with Madeleine at:
www.mhcallway.com
FaceBook: Madeleine Harris-Callway
Twitter: @MCallway
www.mesdamesofmayhem.com

Afterword

by Joan O'Callaghan

The last page has been turned. We trust this romp through the stories in *Thirteen* has left you satisfied and refreshed. Good literature should instruct as well as entertain, and having read all the tales, I believe they accomplish both. It is our hope that, in the process of reading, you were able to laugh, to learn, and to reflect on the kaleidoscopic nature of human behaviour.

We had a wonderful time putting this collection together. In the not-too-distant future, there will be a second one. In the meantime, we invite you to visit the websites and author pages of our contributing writers, and to follow our own exploits at:

http://mesdamesofmayhem.com/.

Mesdames of Mayhem
founder M.H. Callway (centre) and
co-editors Donna Carrick (left)
and Joan O'Callaghan (right)
raise a glass to celebrate the completion of
Thirteen,
An anthology of crime stories
(Carrick Publishing 2013)

Made in United States
North Haven, CT
07 January 2023

30706558R00146